THE GUARDIAN'S FAVOR

BORDER SERIES BOOK NINE

CECELIA MECCA

To Angela and Carolina. Thank you.

CHAPTER 1

ighgate End, Scotland 1274
"Are you going to be ill?" Aidan asked his sister-in-law.

Gillian sat clutching a chamber pot as tenderly as if it were a newborn babe. Her fondness for that pot had been growing of late.

He rushed to her side, pulled her hair behind her back and waited. Aidan had come to the solar looking for his brother. Instead, he'd found Gillian, alone with her chamber pot, looking much as she had every day this past sennight.

"I don't believe so."

Aidan wasn't quite sure he agreed, so he decided to stay put for now. Peering around Gillian's shoulder to see her face, he said, "You don't look good, lass."

"Why thank you. 'Tis kind of you to say, brother."

He should not taunt her, but Aidan could not resist. "The bairn is a wee lassie, no doubt. Another Lyndwood girl come to save the de Sowlis men."

Even as he said it, he could see the color return to Gillian's face. He allowed her hair to fall back against her gown and pulled up a wooden chair to sit beside her. Poor Gillian was often forced to sit, the babe growing bigger inside her every day, and Aidan did not wish to make her feel uncomfortable by towering over her.

"Your brother is convinced otherwise. He believes the babe is a boy."

"His son would be lucky to have such a father."

"Kind words from my brother? To what do I owe the pleasure?" Graeme de Sowlis, clan chief and Aidan's only remaining family member, by blood, walked into the room and strode straight to his wife.

"I'd not have said them had I seen you standing there preening."

Both men knew that statement was not true. Aidan revered his older brother.

"Were you ill?" Graeme knelt beside his wife.

"Nay." She looked into the pot. "Not this time, thank the heavens."

Graeme placed the chamber pot on the floor. When he laid his hand on her slightly rounded stomach, a familiar pang of fear tore through Aidan. This babe, whether it be a nephew or a niece, would not be harmed. If the border descended into chaos, an event some claimed had already happened, they would forsake their family home before they put Gillian and the wee one in danger.

Highgate End may have been the seat of Clan Scott for four generations, but it was nothing more than dirt and stone. If not for the people under their protection, he'd have begged Graeme to take Gillian away. In fact, he'd suggested it once, but his brother had refused to listen.

"You've heard about Douglas?" his brother asked.

"Aye. According to his messenger, the Lord Warden is only a half day's ride from Highgate."

Graeme merely nodded, still crouched beside Gillian.

2

The look on his face was enough to convince Aidan his brother shared his concerns.

Graeme had never hidden his emotions well, his only failing as clan chief. His brother's strength and skill with the sword was unmatched, yet even the most undiscerning adversaries could read his every mood from afar. If he were angry, his foe knew immediately. Now, his worries were written across his face. Worry over the increasing number of raids, the possibility of the first outright battle at the border in years, and the impending arrival of the Lord Warden.

"What do you think he wants?" Graeme stood and began to pace the room.

With more sunlight than most chambers at Highgate Castle, courtesy of an outside wall and two windows whose shutters were currently thrown wide open to usher in the unusually warm April day, the solar had always been the brothers' favored meeting place. Gillian could oft be found in here as well. She liked to imagine the darkness of the long winter was finally behind them, but Aidan feared just the opposite was true.

He shook his head. "I neither know nor want to know. A visit from the Lord Warden now can mean only one thing."

Graeme stopped pacing long enough to stare at him, prompting Gillian to speak up.

"What is it? What's wrong?"

Aidan hated the worry in her voice, but surely she *should* be worried. They all should.

"He would not," Graeme said. His tone did not match his words.

"Why else would he come here now?"

"Would not what? What do you imagine he wants from you?" Gillian asked.

Graeme attempted to explain. "At the council six month earlier, he broached the idea of involving the Earl of Theffield in our dispute with the English border lords."

"The earl," Aidan said, "has property in both England and Scotland."

Graeme's scowl for the man was warranted. Cruel and selfish, the Earl of Theffield tended to elicit such sentiments. Thankfully, he hardly ever visited his northern estates, which were his in name only.

Gillian was rightly confused. "But what has that to do with us?"

"Our father knew the man as well as any Scotsman," Graeme said. "Even though he had no alliance with him and rarely visited Sutworth."

"Sutworth? Isn't that the one that borders our land?"

"Aye." Graeme resumed his pacing, but not before he shot a look at Aidan. Once again, he failed to hide his emotions. The pity in his eyes was as obvious as it was unwelcome.

"But I still don't understand—"

"The Earl of Theffield is Lord Caxton's overlord," Graeme said. "As Caxton's overlord, the Earl of Theffield has the authority to force Caxton to step down."

Lord Caxton, the English Warden of the Middle March, was the reason the Scottish clans had stopped attending the monthly Day of Truce, a day of reckoning for all crimes committed on the border, arbitrated by two wardens, one from either side. Caxton had little interest in fairness, and his willingness to accept bribes and look the other way had allowed too many accused Englishmen to walk free. Until he was removed from his position, the Scottish border lords refused to uphold the tenets of the Treaty of York, which had given them thirty years of relative peace.

The Scottish border lords had tried, and failed, to have Caxton removed from power. Even the intercession of their king had done nothing. The English sovereign had insisted his beloved Lord Caxton would not be removed as warden.

To Gillian, the solution must have seemed inspired—Theffield had land in both Scotland and England, surely he could and would intercede. Her eyes lit up, the possibility of peace at hand, until she looked at him. And Graeme.

"Then why has no one spoken to him yet?"

Aidan did not want to be the one to eradicate Gillian's last hope for peace, so he let his brother do it. "There is a reason Theffield was dismissed as a potential path to peace."

"A good reason," he added.

Gillian studied each of them in turn. "He is that bad then?"

Aidan could not answer. He couldn't think of the man without his fingers itching to grab the dirk at his side and toss it into the closest target.

"Aye, lass," Graeme said. "He is, and worse. Perhaps Douglas has other plans," he added, his voice unconvincing. "Perhaps there is another reason for his visit."

Gillian's chin lifted. "You think he comes to ask you to treat with Theffield?"

Dread filled Aidan's gut. He feared exactly that.

"He asked it once before," Graeme said. "At the council meeting. But while our father knew the man, dealt with him when necessary, neither Aidan nor I have any love for him. But there is no other who would dare approach him. The earl and Douglas nearly killed each other once. The idea was dismissed at the meeting, when there was still hope . . ."

"There is still one thing I do not understand."

He and his brother waited.

"Why do you look at Aidan," she asked Graeme, "as if he lost his favorite dirk? What are you not telling me?"

Before either of them could answer, the color leached out of Gillian's face. She leapt from her seat and grabbed the chamber pot next to her, leaving him thankful not to be forced to answer that particular question.

"Lady Clarissa! We did not expect you."

She tried to smile at the maid she'd known since birth, but even the sight of Eda could not comfort her this day.

"I did not expect to be home so soon." Her back straightened, and she asked, "Is my father in residence?"

Eda's frown confirmed it. The thought that her father might be away from Theffield Castle had been her only solace on the journey back home.

"He is," Eda said, her eyes conveying sorrow, and maybe regret. They were the same emotions she felt for the maid, a woman who had served Theffield faithfully and whose only rewards were the constant demands of a cruel and obstinate master.

"Shall I have your old chamber prepared?" Eda asked as she peered around Clarissa's shoulder. "Are you here alone?"

She'd returned to Theffield without her husband. That simple answer would infuriate her father, the full truth even more so. And though Clarissa trusted Eda as much as she trusted anyone, she would not confide in her until privacy could be ensured.

"Aye," she said simply, hoping her voice sounded more confident than she felt. "Lord Stanley bade me visit out of respect for my father. He would have accompanied me but was called to court just before I left."

As expected, Eda did not question her or accuse her of any falsehoods. Instead, she set in motion the flurry of activity that would be expected upon the arrival of the earl's daughter. Ushered into the hall, Clarissa soon found herself sitting at the head table in front of a goblet of wine and a plate of food, this despite the fact that the midday meal had long since ended. The servants had given her the kind of greeting one might expect from family, and she allowed herself a small smile. It felt good to forget, if only for a moment, this would be anything but a welcome homecoming.

Her father would question her story, of course. He would be disappointed that she'd dared venture beyond her husband's castle walls without the man. But with any luck, he would have no recourse with her errant husband so far south, in London.

According to her, at least.

Clarissa glanced down at her hands, which she'd shoved beneath the table. Willing them to stop shaking, she thought of how much older she felt than when she'd left Theffield nearly two years ago. At twenty and three, she was by no means an old woman. But that did not stop her from feeling like one at times. She'd lived more than one lifetime, it seemed. One as a young, idealistic and hopeful girl who saw herself as the heroine of some great tale, pitted against her father, the villain. And then there was her second lifetime, the hell in which she currently lived. The father she'd hoped to defeat had been replaced with a husband who was equally as bad, or perhaps worse. His only redeeming quality was that he had agreed to set her aside, the blessing that had forced her back home.

"My lady, would you like more wine?"

Had she drunk the first goblet already? Indeed, and eaten her fill as well. Clarissa took a deep, steadying breath, asking the question she did not really want answered.

"Nay, thank you. But if you will," she asked the servant, "do you know precisely when my father will return?"

Clarissa did not have to look up for her answer. As always, his presence made itself known by the reaction of those around her. She knew the signs well. Shoulders tensed. Eyes averted. All, including her, held their breath as the Earl of Theffield entered the hall.

It was not only his height and rigid countenance that made the earl an imposing figure. His cold hazel eyes, flat and emotionless, were the feature most noticed first.

"I cannot say I am glad to see you daughter," he said, each step toward her more menacing than the last. "I'm told you are here without Lord Stanley?"

She watched him approach, waiting. If she spoke too soon,

Clarissa would appear to be acting defensively. Too late, she risked incurring his ire for disrespecting the great Earl of Theffield.

She repeated the lie she'd told Eda. "Lord Stanley bade me come to visit, out of respect for you, Father. He would have accompanied me but was called to court just before I left."

Years of dealing with her father had taught her not to offer more information than was necessary for fear it would be used against her.

"Why?" he demanded quietly.

Servants scattered, and she did not blame them for making themselves scarce. Clarissa only wished she could leave with them. She would never have returned if she'd had anywhere else to go.

"Why did he demand I come or why—"

"Do not"—his voice lowered—"question me."

She lowered her eyes, hoping the gesture would soften his tone. How quickly she had forgotten his dislike of questions. Her father asked, she answered. That was the way it had always been.

"He believed you would wish to see me," she lied. "And I know not his purpose for his journey to London."

She continued to peer down at her hands, willing him to believe her. If he did not . . . if he sent her back . . .

"I do not want you here."

Looking up, Clarissa nearly apologized for her presence. It would have been the smart thing to do, but she could not bring herself to do it. So much had transpired since her marriage, the young woman who'd left Theffield Castle at twenty and one was not the same one who sat here now.

"Of course," she said instead, hoping her tone was appropriately deferential.

It worked. One final grunt, and he walked away.

"I trust you are not staying long," he called back, eliciting looks of pity from those servants who'd been brave enough to remain in the hall. The same looks she'd been receiving her whole life. But their lot was surely worse than hers. They served her father, just as she did, although with no recourse but to do his bidding and accept his verbal abuse.

Do I really have any more recourse than they?

Nay.

But she did, at least, have a plan.

CHAPTER 2

"Tell me," Gillian insisted. Her episode with the chamber pot had done nothing to divert her attention from her question about Theffield and Aidan. She would not stop until she had answers. Ones he was not eager to give.

"'Tis nothing," he equivocated, directing his attention to Graeme. "We do not yet know Douglas's true purpose in being here. Shall we—"

"Nothing?" Gillian cut in, finished with the cleaning cloth and bowl of lavender water. "What is it about Theffield that you're not telling me?" When he stayed silent, her gaze shifted to Graeme.

Graeme would never answer her. It was not his story to tell.

If anyone but Gillian had asked for an explanation, Aidan would have kept silent. But he felt a special kinship with Gillian and her sister Allie that he'd previously only had with Graeme. He loved both women as a brother would, and had vowed to protect them always. The look of disappointment on her face was his undoing.

"Theffield's father," he said, returning to the seat he'd occupied earlier, "was granted Sutworth Manor in the Treaty of York."

So much had changed that day, thirty years ago, when border

lines had finally been drawn. Lands changed hands, the Day of Truce was instituted, and though none had expected the terms to last, they had.

Until now.

"When he died, his son became earl, and Theffield the younger allowed his Scottish estate to languish. Unlike many of the border lords with property in both countries, Theffield had no interest in navigating the complicated landscape of Scotland's border politics. He hardly visited, and when he did, he never took his family. Only once, when I was ten and five, and our father took Graeme and me to meet him . . ."

This is where the real tale began. He'd not spoken of it aloud for two years, and if the pang in his chest were any indication, it would be difficult to do so now.

No more difficult than carrying a child inside your belly as Gillian is. 'Tis simply a story. Tell it.

"There was a girl . . ."

To call her such was imprecise, of course. An angel, he'd thought her at the time. When they'd arrived at Sutworth Manor, the young Lady Clarissa had peeked out from behind her father and was rewarded for her efforts with a stern glare. Aidan had disliked him instantly.

The little lady's round face had stared up at him, innocent bright brown eyes framed with long brown hair. Aidan had wanted to take one of her demurely folded hands and pull her with him, leading her out into the courtyard and beyond. He'd wanted to run as fast and far away as possible from the man who stood by her side . . .

Instead, he'd merely stood beside his father and brother, waiting for the moment when they would be away from the prying eyes of their parents.

"I will see to the preparations for Douglas," his brother said as Aidan realized how long he'd paused his story.

With a final glance back, his brother abandoned him to the

tale. Graeme knew well what happened next, for he had been there the entire time.

"There was a girl?" Gillian prompted.

"Aye, Theffield's daughter."

Aidan leaned forward when Gillian moved her hand to her stomach, worrying she was about to have another bout of sickness, but she waved him away.

"'Tis nothing. Go on."

Bringing himself back to that day, he thought of how quickly he'd developed a dislike for the earl, whom his father had called "the worst sort of man."

"Before our fathers left us to meet, alone, Theffield reprimanded her for coming out to see us and sent her away with a maidservant. Drawn to her, I followed, intending to speak to her, when the girl ran. Away from the maid and directly to the door. It didn't take long to catch her or determine that she intended to run away."

"Poor girl."

"Indeed. She'd not have gotten very far, of course. And I was surprised she opened to me, told me she could no longer endure her father's cruelty. Which, had I not intervened, would have been on display that day."

Aidan recounted how he'd convinced Lady Clarissa of the dangers she would face at such an age were she successful. He told Gillian of the large amount of coin it took to persuade the maid and others who had witnessed the incident to agree to keep it silent.

"I thought often about the desperation that Lady Clarissa must have felt to consider herself safer outside Theffield's walls, alone, than within them."

"Meeting her affected you," Gillian correctly surmised.

"Aye, and Graeme too. She was such a pretty girl, her wide eyes telling us even before we spoke of the difficult life she'd endured. Theffield's daughter was quite sheltered. Meeting us was a novelty for her."

Gillian frowned. He'd not meant to sadden her.

Brought back to the present, Aidan attempted a smile. He did not want to appear a sentimental fool by asking aloud how they'd managed without her for so many years. Lady Gillian's mere presence brightened Highgate End.

Shifting in his seat under Gillian's gaze, he resumed his story.

"Graeme teased me the entire day about the incident. As we were given a tour of the manor, my thoughts were indeed elsewhere."

"On the girl?"

"Aye. Her eyes haunted me that day and for years later until—"

A soft knock at the door interrupted them. Gillian's maid, a young woman nearly as protective of Gillian as he was, entered the room.

"Is there aught you need, my lady?"

"Nay," she said. "As you've likely heard, we are expecting guests. See to them, if you please."

"Aye, my lady. I believe they've already arrived." She bobbed a curtsy and left.

"Until?"

Aidan stood. "Until many years later. It appears Douglas was much closer to Highgate than his messenger anticipated."

He held out his arm. The lady of Highgate End would want to greet their guests.

Gillian took it but did not allow him to pass over the rest of the story so easily. As they walked from the chamber, she prodded him to finish the tale.

"Did you see her again?"

They wound their way through darkened corridors and to a set of circular stairs that led down to the great hall. He deftly avoided answering her question by moving in front of her, a habit he'd gotten into whenever they descended such a tight stairwell.

He did not need to be told a fall in her condition would be detrimental to his wee niece or nephew.

"You did. You saw her. When?"

Taking her arm again as they reached the landing, Aidan delayed for as long as he could without appearing rude. Just as they arrived at the entrance to the hall, he said, "Years later. We ought to greet our guests."

Gillian gave him a look that told him his escape was only a temporary one, and well he knew it.

Escorting her into the hall, Aidan watched his brother, who was speaking to one of the most powerful men in Scotland. A large, fearsome-looking one who would not be waylaid, no matter his request. And when both men looked his way—Douglas with a nod of greeting and Graeme with a look of worry—Aidan already knew the outcome.

They would be traveling south, to Theffield.

Bloody hell.

"My lady?"

Eda entered the chamber hesitantly, as if she were a stranger who had not been there when Clarissa burst into the world, killing her mother in the process. As if she had not been present for the one and only time Clarissa had ever stood up to her father —the argument that had left him red in the face, spitting mad and denouncing her as a daughter.

"Come in, Eda." Clarissa rushed to the doorway and ushered the maid into the chamber.

Pulling a stool away from the whitewashed walls of the bedchamber she had hoped to never see again, Clarissa gestured for Eda to sit, but the maid waved it away.

"My lord would not take kindly to ol' Eda sittin'."

She hated to think it, but the years they'd been apart had not been kind to Eda. More lines ran from the corners of her mouth downward. Eda's features seemed to her more prominent, her wide nose flaring in anger. The fire in her eyes was still there though, the one that had ensured she would never be allowed to follow Clarissa to her new life with Lord Stanley.

"I do not know why you stay."

"And I do not know why you've returned."

Two years apart, and they'd already fallen back into the same argument they'd spent a lifetime debating. It was the first opportunity they'd had to be alone together since Clarissa's arrival the previous afternoon. She'd remained in her chamber until Eda could come to her, knowing the maid would do so as soon as she was able. Cowardly, perhaps, but she had no wish to see her father.

"I thought to tell you last eve—"

"Your father forbade me to come to you."

Clarissa clenched her hands into fists, squeezing with all of her might. The small mutiny did not improve her mood, but she relished the thought of how unseemly her father would think the gesture. "He is a monster."

"Why?" Eda repeated, looking down at Clarissa's hands.

She allowed them to relax and spoke quickly. "Lord Stanley appealed to the ecclesiastical court for a dissolution of our marriage and bade me leave."

Eda looked as if she'd just choked on a fig. "Dissolution? I've never—"

"Nay," she said. "I never did either. Until he broached the topic more than a year ago."

Clarissa thought back to that first conversation. "'Broached' may not be the correct term. More like demanded," she clarified. "Eda," she grabbed the maid's hand, "'twas awful. The physician poked and prodded me—"

When Eda squeezed her hand, Clarissa felt her throat swell with emotion. She did not wish to go into detail about that particular incident. It still haunted her sleep. "But it matters not. When word arrived a sennight past that the dissolution would be allowed, the annulment proceedings could be begun . . ." She shrugged. "Lord Stanley said, ''Tis over. Go home.' And so I did."

There was, of course, much more to tell, but no time to do so. "I will tell you more when we can find another time to speak. Go. And, if you please, send word to Albert that I will be needing his services."

Albert. Her only chance at reaching Sutworth safely. "I do not plan to remain here until Father discovers what has truly happened. And he will, eventually. If I could have convinced Stanley's men to escort me to Sutworth, I'd have done so. But they refused. And so here I—"

She stopped talking, finally seeing the sorrow in Eda's deep brown eyes. The maid's eyes were dark, almost black, and always expressive.

"What is it?"

"I am so sorry, my love."

Nay, not Albert! Please God, no.

"He'd begun to cough—"

Clarissa did not hear the rest. She crumpled onto the stool, head in her hands, and allowed the swelling in her chest to burst. Clarissa had not cried when her father slapped her across the face so hard it had left a red mark for her wedding day. She had not cried after being married to a man nearly as old—and as cruel—as her father.

At least Lord Stanley did not remind her regularly that she killed her own mother. Indeed, the man had hardly spoken to her at all. He'd bought her like cattle and treated her as such. The possibility of an heir was the only reason he'd parted with the land her father had coveted his whole life. She'd been naught but a transaction to them both, and Clarissa had done her duty and married the old man, with nary a tear.

She had not even cried when the king's physician had stuck his fingers inside the most private part of her, verifying she was, indeed, still a virgin. But now, to learn she had lost the one man who had treated her like a daughter, who had risked her father's ire to visit her at Lord Stanley's, and who would have delivered her safely to Sutworth Manor, whence she could flee to Dunburg Abbey . . .

"Nay," she said as Eda gently lowered a hand to her shoulder. Her cheeks and fingers tingled with sorrow as tears continued to flow, the steady stream becoming an aching throb in her chest. "Not Albert, please . . ."

The man had never married, never begat any children. She'd often imagined what life would be like if she were his daughter in truth.

"We will find someone to help," Eda said.

Clarissa wanted to deny those words, but she could not speak. In this moment, she did not care about Sutworth, or Dunburg, or what became of her. Albert was gone, and she didn't get a chance to say goodbye. The only man who'd ever loved her . . . well, not the only man. But Clarissa had ruined that as well. Aidan de Sowlis hated her now, and she did not blame him.

"I do not wish to leave you—"

"Go," she said, looking up, realizing the danger this visit posed for Eda. Wiping her eyes and attempting to smile—a miserable attempt, she was sure—Clarissa pushed the maid away. "I will be fine," she said, not meaning it at all. "Hurry . . ."

"I will be back."

Clarissa returned the smile, wondering how a woman who had served her father her whole life could still manage one. Eda was truly a blessing, a gift from God. She bolted up and tossed her arms around the older woman, squeezing her as Eda chuckled.

"I am sorry." The loss was not only hers, after all.

Clarissa could feel Eda shudder beneath her. Pulling away, she took a deep breath.

"Go," she repeated. Eda did not need a reminder of what her

father would do if she were caught disobeying a direct order. Bobbing a quick curtsy, she left as quietly as she had come.

Clarissa sank back down onto the stool and, for the first time in memory, allowed sorrow to seep into her bones. She would allow herself only a moment of self-pity, just one.

And then it would be time to form a new plan.

CHAPTER 3

*A*idan shifted on his mount, adjusting the leather sheath of the dirk that never left his side. Graeme, at home with Clarissa and their babe, would have enjoyed this challenge. Frowning at the sight before him, he averted his gaze from the looming castle and concentrated instead on the steady pounding of hoofbeats behind him.

As they rode closer, Aidan held up a fist. The men fell into line around him as Theffield Castle came fully into view. Once a motte and bailey castle, it had seen so many additions and renovations that the stronghold was now fully positioned to house an English earl. Unlike the man, Theffield was an impressive holding.

"I'd hoped to never see this place again," Aidan said to no one in particular.

"And I can understand why," Lawrence said beside him.

Lawrence was one of Aidan's closest friends. The son of a chief, he and his clan were more than simply neighbors to Clan Scott. His family, and clan, had been at war with Theffield's neighbors for many years. Lawrence took any opportunity to travel south in hopes of meeting his enemies. In all other dealings,

Clan Karyn sought peace, not war. But the Morley family was one glaring exception.

He and Aidan looked remarkably similar, and had been mistaken for brothers before—a misconception it amused them to indulge. Both had brown hair, though Aidan's was a touch darker, hazel eyes and a hulking build. But the resemblance they bore to each other was nothing compared to that between Aidan and Graeme. He and his brother could pass for twins.

Lawrence looked up into the cloudless sky as a flock of rooks passed overhead. "It seems so long ago when you first met her—"

"I would prefer not to discuss *her*." He'd known the topic would arise eventually, and had little patience for it at the moment. "Thankfully, she will not be in residence," he added, prodding his horse forward.

Unbidden, a memory of Lady Clarissa assaulted him as they rode toward the outer gatehouse of the fortress in front of them. Unlike the young girl he'd described to Gillian, this memory was of a woman, one with the same oval-shaped face and long, straight brown hair. But rather than peeking out from behind her father, this Clarissa leaned over the high wooden stands surrounding the tourney field to offer him a favor. He could still see the creamy skin of the top of her breasts as she strained to tie the simple white ribbon around the tip of his lance.

Another vision assaulted him, the same woman, the same dress. This time, she stood before a glistening Lake Litmere. When he thought of her, he always remembered the beauty of that lake, only outdone by the beauty of the woman. She looked at it, at everything, with such wonder in her eyes.

It was as if she had never seen anything as glorious as that lake before.

Because she hadn't.

With the exception of the infrequent visits she and her father had made to Sutworth Manor, Clarissa had been all but imprisoned within the walls of Theffield Castle. Even so, it had almost defied his belief that she'd never seen a lake before. How was such a thing possible for a woman born and bred in the borderlands? But there was no denying the sheer pleasure of her expression as she dipped her fingers into the frigid water.

"Damn Douglas," he murmured to himself.

"For forcing you to meet with the father or for giving you a reason to remember the daughter?"

They'd slowed their pace as they approached the castle, and apparently Lawrence had heard him.

"Both."

He called up to the guard, then he and his men waited for the drawbridge to be lowered. Theffield's moat had dried out long ago, but that did not prevent use of the ancient drawbridge. It came creaking down, and continued to creak as they made their way across it to the inner bailey.

"You should have sent Graeme," Lawrence said, not for the first time that day.

Though Gillian's babe was not nearly ready to make its entrance into the world, he would never have allowed his brother to travel without him. The chief was needed at home.

"Alec would allow your father to ride alone?" he asked Lawrence.

Lawrence's older brother Alec was their father's second, just as Aidan was Graeme's second, and he would never consider such a thing. They both knew it.

"Alec was never forced to treat with the man responsible for ruining his life."

As guards approached them, Aidan gave his friend a look he hoped would make him stop talking.

"Alec has not spent two years brooding."

"I have not—"

"Greetings, my lords."

Thankful for the interruption, Aidan allowed the reins to be taken from him by a stablehand. Setting aside his irritation, he

21

prepared for the meeting, which promised to be unpleasant at best, deadly at worst.

Theffield was their last hope to bring back the Day of Truce, and with it, peace. If he could not convince the earl to help them, and he doubted very much the man was inclined to do so, the recent skirmishes along the border might escalate to full-scale battles. A discomforting thought indeed.

"My lord is expecting you," another servant said as he led them through the courtyard. "Your men are welcome in the main keep."

He and Lawrence exchanged a glance. It was an odd statement to make, one that implied there had been some discussion about what to do with his men. And obviously a consideration to not allow them in. Though it was the kind of reception he'd expect from the earl, it did not bode well for their meeting.

Theffield was no ordinary keep. Its door, nearly three times the size of most and constructed of old, heavy wood, took two men to open. One pulled the iron handle, and the other pushed from the inside. An elderly man, straining with his efforts, appeared as the door slowly swung open. Like each of the servants that greeted them, his face was dour. Theffield was much as he remembered it . . . without joy. Without light and certainly without love.

Aidan hated it. Hated being here and hated the man who was now walking toward them. His only consolation was knowing the earl had no knowledge of his rendezvous with Clarissa at the Tournament of the North two years earlier. If she had told her father, Aidan would certainly have known about it long ago.

"De Sowlis," the man said, hardly concealing a sneer. "Derrickson."

Though the earl was accustomed to deference, they were no English lords and would not bow as it was not their custom. For a more deserving man, however, he and Lawrence would have done so out of respect. Instead, Aidan extended a hand, which Theffield, not surprisingly, refused to shake.

"Take them to the hall," he ordered of Aidan's men. His rough, dismissive tone was exactly as Aidan remembered it. "You may follow me."

It was unclear whether the invitation had been offered solely to him or also to Lawrence. It did not matter. They would both be going.

"I would bring you to the solar but do not expect this to take long."

Theffield spoke like a man who was accustomed to being in command. And to having those commands followed, no matter how ruthless or ill-advised.

The kind of man who would marry his only daughter to an old man simply to gain a tract of land. But Theffield was not alone in his approach. Men killed, and died, for patches of soil every day. Gillian and Allie could attest to such a fact. Their father had attempted to marry them off well in order to collect the funds to save their home.

Escorting them to a small room off the great hall, much smaller than Aidan would have expected in a castle this size, Theffield seated himself behind the large, flat-topped wooden desk. Its surface was empty but for a single candle in a plain iron holder, its tripod not quite even.

The desk was like the room. Dark and foreboding. Unlike most solar chambers, which allowed for natural light, this one was bathed in shadow barely repelled by the four additional torches on each side of the walls.

"You are here concerning Caxton." It was not a question.

Without being invited to do so, Aidan and Lawrence sat on the high-backed wooden chairs across from Theffield.

"We are," Aidan began. "You have been a neighbor . . ." His tongue stuck on the word *friend*. ". . . to our clan for many years."

Even in the dim light Aidan could see the earl's eyes narrow. "Sutworth. That crumbling pile of stone," he muttered.

In fact, Sutworth was anything but. Its people were rather

resilient in remaining self-sufficient and avoiding conflict, especially considering they had an absentee lord.

"And surely cannot be pleased with the recent turn of events."

A lie, and they both knew it.

If Theffield had wanted to intervene, he would have done so already. Allowing the terms of the treaty to crumble around him, the earl was as responsible as anyone for their current troubles. One word, and he could have Caxton removed from power. Only his English king could make the same claim.

"If you refer to your clans' boycott of the Day of Truce—"

He said the word *clans* as if it were an epithet.

"Because they know the proceedings are no longer fair or just," Lawrence said.

"Know? Or do they merely believe it so?"

Theffield did not betray his emotions, and Aidan did his best to emulate the wily earl. Lawrence was not so composed. "Murderers being set free simply because they are well-positioned?" he said. "'Tis not justice."

Theffield looked at Lawrence, his brows rising. Aidan willed his friend to remain calm, for he knew what was coming.

"It seems you are conveniently forgetting Clan Karyn's bowyer."

Clan Karyn's skilled bowyer, the same man who made every crossbow for Clan Scott, had been accused of murder at an inn just across the border. He'd fled back to Scotland, and since the clans had stopped attending the monthly Day of Truce, he had faced no consequences as of yet.

"My father offered to try the man—"

"In Scotland. On his terms." Theffield's dry, cold laugh sent chills up Aidan's spine. "You truly believe the accused's family would agree to such an arrangement?"

"Enough," Aidan said, risking Theffield's ire.

His friend believed the bowyer had been wrongly accused, but they had not come here to argue the man's guilt or innocence. He could not allow the incident to become a distraction.

"We are here to discuss Caxton."

Theffield slammed his hands on the table before him and leaned forward. "Give me one reason I should oust my own man, against the wishes of our king, to help you," he spat.

"Not to help me, or Clan Karyn. But to take our only remaining chance at peace. With Lord Caxton in power, the chiefs will not allow their clans to be subjected to one-sided justice. Without the Day of Truce, the reivers will once again be allowed free rein, and the hard-won peace of the last thirty years will have been for naught. Is that truly what you desire, my lord?"

Aidan also sat forward, meeting the earl's defiant position with his own.

"Tell me, Theffield. Is that what you want?"

He could not understand the man. He had as much at stake in this matter as any border lord, more with lands on both sides of the border, and yet he distanced himself from it.

"Are you not Lord Caxton's overlord?" he pressed.

The insult was intended. But surprisingly, Theffield did not appear insulted. Instead, he sat back and crossed his arms.

"What are Douglas's terms?"

The only question that mattered.

"Force Caxton to step down. In return, Douglas will agree to move the Truce Day here."

Theffield, known for his cool, detached demeanor, failed to contain his surprise. The Day of Truce had been held across the border, in Scotland, since its inception. It had been part of the original bargain, and such a contested term that it had nearly torn apart the treaty before it was signed. In truth, only some of the clan chiefs had agreed to these new terms, but Theffield did not need to know as much.

"Here? At Theffield?"

Aidan forced himself not to show any surprise. The bastard was actually going to agree.

A movement just outside the door caught the man's attention before anything further was said. By the time Aidan turned to look, there was nothing there. Whatever, or whomever, it was, Theffield didn't like it. He stood and waved Aidan and Lawrence from the room.

"We are done here. I will send word of my decision."

It was the best they could have hoped for, and better than being tossed out before they could share their terms.

"You will understand," Theffield said as he led them from the chamber, "why I will not ask you to remain at the castle."

Aidan was sure he could not manage to eat in the presence of this man, so he would have it no other way.

"We did not expect otherwise," he said, the barb hitting its mark.

With a scowl at them both, Theffield turned them over to the same man who'd escorted them into the hall.

"Good day," he said, clearly not meaning the words.

"And to you, my lord," Lawrence said, catching Aidan by surprise. His friend was rarely this gracious to someone so lacking in manners. Then again, it appeared they were on the cusp of an agreement. The smart thing to do would be to pacify Theffield.

Saying his own farewell, Aidan was about to step back through the ridiculously large door leading outside when he saw a flash of bright yellow, unmistakable for its contrast to the darkness that otherwise consumed the hall. The person who'd distracted the earl in his solar.

Ignoring the movement, and Theffield's reaction to it, Aidan stepped outside and back into the sunlight. But he couldn't help but wonder who lurked in the shadows of the hall? And why did the hair on his arms suddenly stand up straight, as if . . .

Nay. It could not be.

CHAPTER 4

*A*t first, Clarissa couldn't breathe. When Eda had told her Aidan de Sowlis was in her father's solar in Theffield, she had not believed it. To say his presence was unexpected would be too mild. It was as shocking as it would be to wake up to a loving smile from her father. Besides which, Eda had never actually met Aidan. Though she'd been at Sutworth Manor when Aidan visited with his brother and father, she'd taken ill that morn and had only heard of the incident from Clarissa herself.

Poor Eda used to lament how many times she'd been forced to listen to the tale of the two handsome Scotsmen. In particular, Clarissa had talked about the younger son, the one who'd looked at her with a mixture of awe and pity. The one she'd continued staring at from afar after she was reprimanded for being in the hall despite having been ordered to stay away from visitors.

And, of course, Eda had not been present at the tournament. It was a wonder Clarissa had been allowed to attend. No amount of begging ever convinced her father to relent, but that time, a stroke of pure luck—or perhaps fickle fate—had sent her uncle and cousin to Theffield just before the tournament. Her cousin, the eldest son of her father's only brother, did the begging for her.

When her father agreed to allow her to accompany them, Clarissa had never been so happy in her life.

Nay, that was not true.

Her happiest day came later in the week when she shared her first kiss with the man who had haunted her dreams for years after his visit to Theffield.

Careful not to be seen by her father, Clarissa peered inside her father's solar. Despite the danger of being caught, she hadn't been able to stay away. She bit back a gasp. Though she could only see the back of his head, it was enough to know it was indeed Aidan de Sowlis. She'd recognize him anywhere.

But why was he here? And who was he with? She couldn't discern whether it was Aidan's brother, but she was not daft enough to remain in the doorway and risk getting caught by her father. Instead, she fled to her bedchamber, looking for Eda along the way, but the maid was nowhere to be found.

Perhaps it was better this way. If Eda knew what she was planning, the maid would be forced to lie when asked about her whereabouts. This way, Eda would be telling the truth. Though she knew the abbey was Clarissa's intended destination, by way of Sutworth, she didn't know anything about her escape plan.

Without time to do more than gather a sack with a few garments stuffed inside, Clarissa walked as quickly as possible without garnering undue attention, finally exiting a side door that led to the inner bailey. There were very few loyal to her father, but those who were would not hesitate to tell him his daughter had been sneaking around the castle clutching a satchel to her chest.

With her heart hammering at the thought of what she was about to do, Clarissa avoided notice as best she could and waited. Of all her foolhardy plans, this was by far the riskiest. If her father caught her attempting to leave with the Scotsman . . .

But what worried her most was Aidan's reaction.

Clarissa managed to make her way to the outer bailey without raising suspicion. However, assuming Aidan *did* agree to escort her to Sutworth Manor, she could not simply ride out through the main gatehouse with him and his companion. At least not without risking that her father's men would recognize her and drag her back inside. Thankfully, this April day was cool enough to warrant a hooded cape, which she'd managed to secure before leaving. Slipping it on and tugging the hood as low on her face as possible, Clarissa waited in a small alcove along the inner curtain wall.

Only an empty, grassy courtyard, a gatehouse full of watchmen, and the man she'd once spurned stood between her and freedom.

Or temporary freedom, at least.

Even if she did manage to reach Sutworth, so much could still go wrong. Just one member of the household with enough loyalty to her father would alert him to her presence at Sutworth. And there was still the matter of getting to Dunburg Abbey. One did not simply arrive at an abbey and ask to be offered admission. Though she carried with her enough jewelry to offer as a dowry, she would still need to find a sponsor. Ideally, the sponsor would be her father, but he had no idea she'd been cast aside by her husband, let alone that she planned to join the order of Benedictine nuns at Dunburg. Nor would he ever allow it. Father Patrick, Sutworth's kindly priest, would be the man to decide her fate.

When Clarissa thought of all that could go wrong, she began to worry. But she'd needed a miracle for her plan to work, and it would seem she had one. Best that she take advantage of it.

Unfortunately, as the Scotsman and his companion rode through the inner gatehouse, fierce and foreboding, they looked less like angels than they did the devil's henchman. As they rode toward her position, followed at a short distance by their men, Clarissa nearly changed her mind. This was madness. After everything that had passed between them, it was unthinkable to ask a favor of him. One that might put him in a great deal of danger.

But she had no choice.

As the hoofbeats thundered closer, Clarissa clutched her satchel, using the material gathered between her fingers to steady her shaking hands. Staring in shock—his hair was much shorter but still curled in waves atop his head—Clarissa moved as if her feet were stuck in the mud beneath them. Slowly making her way to a position that would force them to stop, she released her grip on the satchel with one hand and raised it into the air.

Just as she'd planned, the men slowed, and then stopped, their mounts in front of her. She had precious little time, the risk of being recognized by her father's people very real. Watching as his eyes widened in recognition, Clarissa was brought back to the second time they'd seen each other. He'd caught her staring at him on the jousting field. Embarrassed, she had looked away. Only when he'd later called up to the stands to ask for her favor had Clarissa allowed herself another glance.

That time, his square jaw and kindly smile had taken her breath away. But he was certainly not smiling now. Quite the opposite, in fact. Aidan de Sowlis looked at her as if she were the last person in the world he wanted to be looking at. Lifting her chin and attempting to keep her voice from quavering, she spoke quickly.

"Help me" was all she managed. It was far from the eloquent speech she'd practiced, and it conveyed none of the information she'd hoped would appeal to the honor which she knew he had in abundance. Clarissa had planned to quickly explain that she needed his escort, without which her father would either cast her out as her husband had done or promptly promise her to another equally wretched potential husband.

But no other words came out.

Luckily, it seemed she did not need them. Whether it was the fear in her eyes or something else that had moved him, Clarissa didn't have time to guess. In the swiftest of movements, he reached down and lifted her up as easily as if she were a small lad.

He didn't speak, but instead pulled her toward him, reaching around to twist the reins about his hand.

As quickly as they had stopped, he and his companion were once again moving.

The shock of being in Aidan de Sowlis's arms again was barely tempered by her terror of being recognized by her father's guards.

Dipping her head down, Clarissa closed her eyes and prayed. She pleaded with God to allow them to pass, promising to devote her life to him in exchange for safe passage and to never again disobey him. She apologized for cursing him when she'd been led to the altar to marry Lord Stanley.

"Please, please, please . . ."

She hadn't even realized she'd said the words aloud until a low voice from behind her broke her fervent prayer.

"You can stop now, lass."

Clarissa opened her eyes. The drawbridge had been lowered before they approached, as was the custom at this time of the day, and they rode across it now. The gatehouse was already behind them. They rode past a merchant who traveled in the opposite direction in a covered wagon. Otherwise, they saw no one ahead of them. Just open fields and grassy knolls.

She'd done it!

"And I'll be wanting an explanation as well."

Clarissa didn't dare look back. Where to even begin?

"Greetings, Aidan," she said instead.

"That, my lady, best be the beginning of a very detailed account of what the hell just happened."

KEEPING his voice as even as possible given the circumstances, Aidan attempted to put as much distance as possible between himself and the woman whose backside was currently wedged against him. He'd asked for an explanation, but really he wanted much, much more.

"'Tis a long story," she began hesitantly.

Though he couldn't see her face, Aidan could sense her unease. Despite the fact that Theffield Castle was her family home, Aidan had scarcely believed it was her standing there, waving her satchel. It had taken his mind a moment to reconcile what his eyes told him. Not only was Clarissa standing before him, but he knew at once the lady was desperate. The terrified look on her face had been enough to cut through his shock, and he hadn't hesitated to scoop her up. But that shock had begun to ease, giving way to so many other emotions he could hardly keep track of them. He needed to understand why he'd just abducted her from Theffield.

"Aidan, what in God's name—"

He shot Lawrence a look and then glanced back at the others. His friend understood the silent request and dropped back to ride with the other men. He could only imagine what Lawrence must be thinking.

"You were saying?"

She turned her head then, and God help him, Aidan's breath caught. Though the hood covered the top portion of her head, dipping over her eyebrows, every other feature was on full display, as if he'd not already memorized them. A perfectly oval face, smooth cheeks and full lips. Though he couldn't see it, Aidan imagined her brown hair, parted down the middle and pulled off her face as it had been each time he'd seen her. And though she quickly looked away, turning her head back toward the road in front of them, her eyes haunted him. Just like that first time, the liquid amber shone with a brightness he'd not expect in the Earl of Theffield's daughter.

"I beg you give me escort to Sutworth Manor."

Aidan thought she would continue, but his riding companion offered no further explanation. Ignoring his body's response to her, one he had no right to have toward a married woman, he said, "I will need more than that, as I'm sure you understand, Lady Clarissa."

"I will explain all, of course. But please say you'll do it. I would never ask such a thing if I were not desperate."

Of course she would not. Lady Clarissa was the only daughter of one of the most powerful English border lords. She could call upon any number of men for assistance, if she so chose, but was asking *him* for escort. A man whom she'd brought to his knees, twice.

"An odd request, I'm sure you will admit?"

Her shoulders stiffened. If that insulted her, then Lady Clarissa would not want to hear his opinions on how they'd parted two years earlier. He had no difficulty conjuring that moment, the one that had left him alone on the shores of Lake Litmere, waiting for hours, while his forfeited match was awarded to another participant. He'd assumed something had kept her away, but he'd returned to the tents to find her gone. No trace of the Earl of Theffield's daughter.

She didn't answer him now, and Aidan had nothing more to say. He could refuse to go any further without an explanation. He could demand, as he'd wanted to do for years, to know what had happened that day, and why she had torn his heart from his very chest.

Instead, he fell silent, answering her without speaking.

He would not deny a woman who pleaded for help. Even this woman.

Especially this woman.

When a pair of Galloways appeared atop the ridge in front of them, Aidan raised a fist in the air. His men quickly caught up with him, and Lawrence appeared at his side.

"Do you recognize them?" Lawrence asked.

Their distinct ponies marked them as reivers, but as the men approached, Aidan shook his head. He had not come across these two before. "Nay, but there appears to be only the pair of them."

It was unusual for border reivers to travel in small numbers, so they waited, and watched, to see if others would appear. When they did not, and the reivers rode by them, a nod and wave their only greeting, Aidan took his hand from the dirk at his side.

"Two," Lawrence said. "Most unusual."

Though he agreed, he did not wish to further alarm Clarissa. "They don't appear to pose a threat," he said.

Lawrence looked over at them, the question in his eyes one Aidan couldn't yet fully answer. He knew of Clarissa, of course, but never met her before. His friend had not attended the Tournament of the North that year. The chief of Clan Karyn, Lawrence's father, had taken ill. Though he had recovered, Lawrence had missed the one opportunity each year for Scottish warriors and English knights to come together and fight, as peaceably as possible. Deaths still occurred each year, as they did at all tournaments, but it was a tradition that brought people together across the border—one that would be jeopardized by a breakdown of the peace.

Unless her father deemed it in his interest to help them. An unlikely event if he discovered Aidan had absconded with his daughter.

Pushing the disturbing thought aside, he indicated for the men to keep moving. They hadn't traveled very far when he heard the faintest of whispers.

"I'm sorry."

She'd not turned around, but Aidan heard the words distinctly.

He didn't want to know, he told himself. It mattered naught. She was married. And he would never be. So when he blurted out, "Why?" it was a surprise even to himself.

She wiggled forward, Aidan swallowing hard at the movement, and reached up to remove her hood. The moment she did, a mass of straight brown hair was revealed. He didn't mean to inhale, but the scent of roses assaulted him.

She turned to him then, and if a band of fifty reivers had come at them in that moment, Aidan wouldn't have had the composure to reach for his sword. He did not know what he'd done to deserve this. But God was punishing him, to be sure.

"I wanted to come that day," she began. "To meet you . . ."

He thought, for the briefest of moments, he wanted to hear this. But he simply couldn't bear it.

"Lawrence," he called. His friend appeared by their side moments later. Aidan slowed to a stop, lifted Clarissa from her position nearly on his lap, and lowered her to the ground. As soon as she realized what he was about, she eagerly assisted him. It seemed he wasn't the only one anxious to put distance between them.

Then perhaps you should have asked another for assistance.

Just as he was about to tell Lawrence to take her, Aidan changed his mind.

"Tell the men to get off the road."

There was nothing to recommend this as a good place to stop. No water for the horses or even cover for the men. But he could not simply keep riding toward the border without knowing what the hell was happening with Clarissa.

Handing his reins to his confused companion, Aidan walked a short distance away, turning back to Clarissa, who lifted her gown and followed.

"I will know. Now."

She swallowed. "I made a grave mistake," she said, her voice shaky. "Instead of keeping it secret, as we agreed—"

"Not that." His voice had a hard edge he scarcely recognized. Aidan had always been able to command attention without raising his volume. He was respected despite it, or maybe because of it. But she had the ability, it seemed, to bring out a part of him that he wasn't sure he liked.

"This." He gestured around them.

"As I said, I will explain—"

"You will explain now."

Did she really expect him to bring her to Sutworth Manor without so much as a hint of explanation?

"But we must not tarry. If my father—"

"If your father learns the very man who just begged him to oust Lord Caxton as warden has made off with his only daughter, there will be bigger troubles than this region has seen in years."

Her eyes went as wide as two round trenchers. "He would never . . ."

"He would never what?"

Aidan didn't like where her thoughts seemed to be headed.

"Never mind."

Clasping her hands in front of her, Clarissa continued. "Lord Stanley appealed for an annulment. He cast me out, and my father does not yet know. I came home only because I had nowhere else to go. In order for my plan to work, I must get to Sutworth Manor. I didn't know how I'd manage such a feat, but then you arrived—"

He heard the words, but could not believe them.

"Lord Stanley *what?*"

"He appealed for annulment. I know not how long these things take, but apparently it has already been—"

"I don't believe it."

Blood pounded in his ears, the words coming from her mouth . . .

Nay, it could not be.

"Why would he—"

"Aidan, please. I know you must be angry with me—"

"I stopped being angry with you a long time ago."

It was not true, of course. But he felt as if he should say it anyway.

"If my father finds me here . . ."

Panic. Fear. Of course she was afraid. Better men than him shook at the very mention of the Earl of Theffield. That bastard was Lady Clarissa's father, though Aidan had never quite reconciled himself to that fact.

Annulled.

Pushing aside the implications of that word, Aidan reached out and grabbed Clarissa's hand, wishing immediately he'd not done so. When they touched, a warmth spread through him, the same jolt he'd felt the last time her skin was pressed to his own.

Ignoring the dangerous thought, he guided her back to the men. But just as he was about to lift her onto his mount, Aidan remembered the torture he'd been through since Theffield Castle. He gently pushed her toward Lawrence, who didn't need to be told what to do. As he helped her mount, pulling his hands from her waist as if they were on fire, he cursed himself for the musings that danced through his mind.

It didn't matter if she would no longer be a married woman. She'd abandoned him without so much as a goodbye. She was the daughter of the only man remaining who had the power to bring peace to the border. One who would surely be enraged to find his daughter missing.

An annulment did not matter.

Except that it did.

CHAPTER 5

*U*nlike with Aidan, she sat behind his companion, who had introduced himself simply as Lawrence. Holding on to his waist as he'd instructed, she tried to pretend it was normal for her to ride astride a horse with a strange Scotsman. She'd only been this close to a man six times in her life—precisely three times when her husband had attempted to beget a son with her, the day Aidan had kissed her, earlier when she had sat in front of him, and now. And while her body did not flush with warmth as it did whenever Aidan de Sowlis was near, neither did it recoil in fear as it always had with her husband.

No longer afraid they would be caught any moment, Clarissa allowed herself to consider what would happen next. At least, she attempted to do so, but every time she conjured Sutworth Manor or the priest who she prayed would help her, Clarissa found herself glancing to her right.

He never once looked her way. His profile may have scared her had she not known the type of man he was. Not that she knew Aidan well, but there was no mistaking his kind nature.

Though he did not look very kindly now.

"Who are you?"

It was not asked with heat but out of curiosity.

"Lady Clarissa of Theffield."

The man, Lawrence, whipped his head to the side and glanced at her briefly before turning his attention back to the dirt road in front of him. Covered with gravel that kicked up every so often, the land was at least flat. It had been so long since she'd traveled north, to Sutworth, that only small portions of the journey remained in her memory.

"*You* are Lady Clarissa?"

He knew her father, of course. It likely surprised him that she would be here with them rather than back at Theffield Castle. Or with her husband.

"Aye," she said dispassionately. Accustomed to the various reactions people had upon learning of her association with Theffield, Clarissa attempted to ignore his tone.

"Lady Clarissa."

Was she expected to respond?

"I thought you were married to—"

"Aye, I am." She preferred not to hear her husband's name spoken aloud.

"Then what . . . why?" He stopped. "Holy hell and the blessed mother, what have we done?"

Again, no response seemed appropriate, so Clarissa chose to remain silent.

His looks and countenance reminded her a bit of Aidan, which was perhaps why she'd told him as much as she had. Clarissa hoped he would not ask further questions, and her prayers were answered. They rode until the sun began to set. And though her bottom was beginning to get sore and her stomach rumbled, Clarissa did not utter a sound. These men had saved her, and she would be eternally grateful. She'd die before she opened her mouth to utter a complaint.

Finally, when she'd begun to despair that Aidan would never look at her, he glanced over at them. She tried to tell herself she was not disappointed when she realized he did not intend to address her.

"We cannot ride through the night."

He'd reared his horse nearly to a stop.

When he did look at her, Aidan did not appear pleased. It occurred to her that their plans must have changed because of her presence.

"The Wild Boar is behind us, and Anvil Inn too far out of the way," Lawrence said.

"We go to Sutworth Manor first."

Now that they had stopped, Lawrence turned completely around to stare at her. She blinked but refused to look away under his close scrutiny.

"Aidan, we really should not—"

"It is not negotiable."

"Staying somewhere along the road is much too risky. Tensions are too high . . ."

"We'll stop," Aidan said, appearing to make a decision, "feed and water the horses, and then ride." He shifted his gaze to her. "Can you do that, Clarissa?"

Two things happened at once when he said her name. Clarissa's heart began to race and she noticed Lawrence did not flinch. As the daughter of an earl, few would call her by her given name. Even family members did not always do so, at least not without using her title.

Which meant Aidan's friend knew what had passed between them at the tournament.

Trying not to appear embarrassed, she said to Aidan, "I can do it."

Her backside screamed in protest. Clarissa's husband had taken her father's advice and did not allow her far from the castle, which meant any rides she'd taken had been rather short. But these men did not need to know that.

He seemed pleased by her declaration. With a shout from Aidan, they rode on until marshland turned into a patch of trees.

"There," he shouted again, and everyone came to a stop. Dismounting, Lawrence lifted her off his horse and set her gently onto the ground. She eyed the tree line longingly, and when some of the men brought their mounts into the thicket, Clarissa ached to follow. But how exactly did one ask delicately to relieve themselves?

"Come with me."

Aidan appeared from behind her, and she was more than happy to comply. He didn't speak as he led her deeper into the dark woods, the sound of running water not far from them. Presumably, it was why they'd stopped here.

"You may use the high bushes there."

Swallowing her fear, Clarissa moved toward them as if being enveloped in darkness in the middle of a dense forest in the borderlands were something she'd done many times before.

She finished quickly, relieved to find Aidan just where she'd left him.

Dressed in a simple tunic and trewes, his ever-present dirk strapped to his side, he looked more like a warrior than a knight. Which, of course, he was.

"Are you hungry?"

She nodded. In fact, she'd not eaten all day, and hardly at all the day before.

"Come," he said, turning back toward the others, "I have—"

"Wait."

When he did as she asked, Clarissa immediately regretted the simple word. Though every part of her wanted to pour out her story, tell him what had happened that night, why she never came . . . the look on his face stopped her. He was not angry, precisely, but nor was there any special regard in his gaze. He stared back at her as if she were a woman like any other, waiting only because she'd commanded him to do so.

"I wanted to thank you," she began. Once again, it was a different speech than the one she'd intended, but the words needed to be said. "I know you take a risk to escort me—"

"Lass, if you knew the risk, you'd not have asked for this."

What was she supposed to say to that?

"Douglas hoped our neighborly ties would endear your father to me more than most—"

She laughed, not meaning to do so. "My father is endeared to no one."

If she had been born a boy, perhaps things would have been different. Or if she'd not "killed her mother coming into the world."

"As you say, but he gave my clan the burden anyway."

The burden of treating with her father. "You hope he will convince Lord Caxton to step down as warden?"

She'd met the English Warden of the Middle March on more than one occasion. And while she would never presume to know a man's intentions, it did not seem likely this one would step down willingly. A favorite of the king, his reputation was as a man who enjoyed skirting the law . . . not one who cared about the opinion of the Scots across the border.

"Nay," he said, "to force him to do so."

She'd have laughed again, but Aidan appeared to be serious.

"He will not do it," she said with conviction. "My father—"

"This is the last chance at peace."

"But he is one man. Surely—"

"We must get back." He turned from her once again.

Before she could think better of it, Clarissa's hand shot out to grab his arm. "But wait—"

He did not attempt to remove her hand, and she did not wish to pull away.

But when he looked at her as if she were the barrier between his clan's safety and all-out war, her hand did drop.

He hated her.

The man who'd once leaned down to kiss her with such reverence, giving her the happiest memory of her entire life . . . he hated her, and Clarissa did not blame him.

"I'm sorry," she repeated.

For stupidly telling her father she had met a man, an action she'd regretted every day since . . . for leaving him, and the tournament, though it had not been her choice to do so. For putting him, his clan, and all of the borderlands at risk. For all of it. Clarissa was so, so sorry for everything that had happened between them.

That mistake had cost her everything, and she'd paid for it every day since.

He did not answer. Instead, he turned and walked away.

Clarissa was forced to follow or risk being attacked by one of the unknown animals or reivers or whatever was back there in the woods behind her.

She deserved his scorn. Deserved all that had happened to her since that day . . .

The pain in her chest was so great that when a shout was raised, when Aidan began yelling back to her, it took her some time to come out of the sorrowful reverie.

When the fog of self-pity finally lifted, Clarissa realized what was happening.

They were under attack.

AIDAN PULLED CLARISSA back into the brush and down to the ground.

"Stay here," he whispered, "and do not move."

He could tell she was terrified, but there was no time to comfort her. Running toward the sound, Aidan assessed the situation, dirk in hand. There were four men he could see. One, weapon drawn, engaged Lawrence, while the others had yet to dismount. But they did so quickly, just as he arrived in the clearing.

When one of the other reivers charged his friend from behind, his hand raised to stab him, Aidan didn't think. He aimed and threw his dagger directly at the assailant's shoulder. The man's immediate cry of pain told him he'd met his mark. At the same time, Aidan's other men arrived on the scene and descended on the reivers, all six ready to fight. Those still mounted bolted. The one he'd injured did the same, looking in his direction before he rode away.

Only one of them remained, though he dropped his sword as the Scott clansmen surrounded him.

"What happened here?" Aidan asked.

The reiver panted from his efforts with Lawrence.

"They attacked without cause," Lawrence said. "I know not the reason."

Aidan turned toward the reiver. "Who are you?"

The dark-bearded man refused to answer. He glared at him as if offended Aidan had dared ask such a question.

"English or Scot?"

Without a Day of Truce, justice would be served now if the man was English. If he was a Scot, he would be granted a trial. One that would likely result in his death.

"Scot," he finally answered.

Today only, perhaps.

Border reivers tended to claim allegiance to whatever country suited them. But he did not want to waste time deciphering the truth of the man's statement. He needed to get back to Clarissa.

"He cannot travel with her," Aidan said. Lawrence must have already come to the same conclusion. He'd already fetched rope from his saddlebag, with which he proceeded to tie the man's hands behind his back.

"I will take him. For the offense of attacking a member of Clan Karyn," he said. The man's wild-eyed reaction confirmed he was indeed Scottish. Clan Karyn's reputation was widespread. Even the Highlanders knew enough to stay away from them in a fight. And though he did not know the reason for the man's attack, Aidan did know what his fate would be.

"Take one of my men . . ."

"No."

Lawrence would be stubborn on this. "You will not travel alone with a murderer."

"I refuse—"

"Do you imply I need so many men to guard me?"

He had him, and his friend knew it. Glowering at him, Lawrence nonetheless extended his hand to Aidan.

"Until we meet again."

Aidan shook it, the firm squeeze a reminder of Lawrence's strength. "Thank you for accompanying me. He nodded toward the trees. "I must go . . ." Turning to address his men, he said, "One of you, go to Clan Karyn. The rest of you, back to back."

The warning to be on alert was hardly needed. His men knew what to do. Running back toward Clarissa, he found her exactly as he had left her. Alone and scared.

Squatting down next to her, he said, "It's over."

He understood the tears that sprang to her eyes. Knowing her father, he did not doubt this was the first time she'd been involved in any sort of attack.

She was shaking, and Aidan didn't blame her. He stood, lifting her with him. Without thinking, he pulled her to him and wrapped his arms around her.

This could be Gillian, or Allie. Another sister. She simply needs comfort.

Hell . . . she didn't feel like a sister. Clarissa felt as she had the only other time he'd held her this close.

Damn good.

Too good.

"I . . . I don't know why—"

Resisting the urge to move his hand up far enough to feel her glossy hair, Aidan said, "It is done. Scottish reivers, one in custody, the others fled. They will not hurt you."

It would take a bit longer for her body to catch up with her mind's reaction. As soon as Clarissa realized she was indeed safe, they needed to get back on the road.

He waited, trying to pretend holding her this way had no effect on him. Trying to pretend the way her small hands clasped his tunic did not make him feel stronger and more powerful.

"I'm sorry." Her words were mumbled against his chest. She pulled away then, wiping her eyes and looking at him as if seeing him for the first time. "I did not mean—"

He released her and stepped back. Aidan had no choice. He could not be this close to her.

"The first time my father, brother, and I were attacked on the road," he said, "was on this very journey south. I thought I was well prepared, but by the time the skirmish ended, I had not stepped but a short distance away from my mount. My father and his men, including my brother, dispatched three English reivers to God in the same time it took me to dismount."

He hated that particular memory. Aidan had not had the opportunity to atone for his inaction for several more years.

"There is no shame in being unprepared for death," he continued.

Their eyes met.

He did not need the moonlight to know her eyes were the most extraordinary shade of brown, like darkened liquid gold. Everything he'd felt for her in the past was still there. The months he'd spent cursing her after the tourney didn't matter. Nor did the torment he'd endured upon learning she was married. Nor did the fact that she was *still* married.

He stepped back, as if burned.

"Lawrence is taking our hostage back with him," he said, walking away. Hearing the crunch of twigs behind him, he continued. "You'll ride with me. If you tire, sleep. By the time the sun rises, we should arrive at Sutworth Manor."

She would be in the care of others. No longer his concern.

"I would like to explain—"

"I would prefer you did not."

It no longer mattered why she had left the tournament without a word. He'd assumed the reason had something to do with her father.

But that was in the past. He had moved on. Resigned himself to seeing his brother happy. To being a brother to his two new sisters, who had graced his life with joy.

He cared not for her explanations, for they changed nothing. And to ensure she did not have an opportunity to change his mind, he would have her ride with one of his men.

Pleased with himself, Aidan led her into the clearing, looked at the remaining men, and tried to decide which of them would not need to be reminded of her status as a married woman.

Goddammit.

CHAPTER 6

*C*larissa startled herself awake. It was still so dark she could barely see anything beyond the horse's ears, though it was clear they no longer rode through deep woods. Moorland, Aidan had called it before she drifted off. With a small smile, she closed her eyes again. When he'd told her to close her eyes, to rest, she'd adamantly insisted such a thing would not be possible. Clarissa had difficulty falling asleep even in the comfort of a soft feather bed. Surely she'd not be able to do so riding atop a horse in the arms of, well, him.

"Sleep well?"

The voice was polite but void of any emotion.

"Surprisingly so."

They were the first words he'd spoken to her since he'd helped her mount. She'd assumed he was annoyed by her presence, so she'd stopped trying to think of what to say. Of how to explain something he did not want an explanation for. Eventually, she'd fallen asleep, his arms wrapped around her and gripping the horse's reins. His hands were like two lanterns in an otherwise darkened room.

"Where are we?" she murmured, opening her eyes again. It was no use attempting to fall back asleep. She was too aware of him behind her.

"In friendly territory."

Scotland then.

"Not far from the southernmost border of your father's land."

He did not attempt to hide the contempt in his voice, but Clarissa didn't blame him. Sutworth deserved more than an absentee lord who cared little for its people. But such were the ways of the border—allegiances and property ownerships changed nearly as often as the weather.

Her chest constricted at the thought of the risk he'd taken to bring her here. He deserved at least one more attempt at the truth.

"I told him."

He stiffened around her, but she continued her explanation. The words needed to be said. Aidan de Sowlis was a good man, one she'd hurt, though not on purpose.

"I told my father I had met someone. Begged him to consider meeting you."

Clarissa braced for it.

"Pardon?"

"I should not have done so, of course. I should have met you, as planned. But I was filled with the excitement of a young woman . . ." She'd almost said a young woman in love. The sentiment was certainly not one he'd appreciate.

"I'd wondered why he'd allowed me to attend the tournament at all, the same man who'd refused to allow even a simple ride outside our walls. I thought he'd simply yielded to my uncle's persuasion. But then Father mentioned Lord Stanley was in attendance." Warming to her topic, Clarissa rushed to finish. "As soon as I understood his reason for bringing me, that Stanley was there to get a closer look at 'the prized mare,' I had to do something. So I told him. And we left. More precisely, I was forced to leave."

She did not dare turn around to see his face. She'd lived with the consequences of that bad decision for two years. It had been a horrible, horrible mistake, and she knew it

And so she waited. And waited. And waited. So long, in fact, that Clarissa wondered if he had fallen asleep, though of course that could not be possible. Finally, she could not take it any longer. She turned her head, and immediately wished she hadn't.

It was worse than him being horrified.

Aidan looked completely unaffected. As if she'd just told him it was dark outside. Or that she was English.

Nothing.

His lips flattened. "Hmm."

That was it?

She looked away, her heart sinking to her shoes. A comment on her stupidity would have been preferable.

He'd told her he did not want her explanation, that he no longer cared. Perhaps she should have believed him.

"You never sent word."

So much time had passed since his "hmm" that it took a moment for Clarissa to realize what he meant.

"If I'd had the means to do so, I would have."

"The means . . . you could not have found—"

"You don't know my father very well." She chanced a glance back, taking in his flexed jaw and his unreadable eyes. "There were precious few at Theffield I could entrust with such a message, and even fewer who had the means to leave my father without an explanation."

She wished she'd not looked back. Or attempted to explain. Though she could not wish he had not appeared to rescue her, for if Aidan hadn't whisked her onto his horse, she never would have made it this far.

"I just thought you should know."

"And Stanley?"

Every time she thought him disengaged, Aidan surprised her with another question.

"We were married less than a sennight later."

This time, his silence was not punctuated by more questions. This time, he said nothing more, and Clarissa offered the same. Her marriage—or her father's betrayal, as she liked to remember it—was not a topic she ever wished to discuss. Clarissa knew how lucky she was that her husband had wanted a son from her, so badly, in fact, that he had used his substantial influence to obtain an annulment so he could marry a more fertile bride.

She shuddered at the thought of spending a lifetime with that man.

Clarissa was lucky indeed, and she would not waste another moment wishing for more. She'd obtained absolution from a man she'd never expected to see again. Hoping for a future she would never have would serve no purpose.

But she was not chattel.

Clarissa was a lady nobly born, one who carried a satchel of jewels she'd never cared about, until now. And those would buy her the only future she dared to consider.

DAMN.

Aidan repeated the word in his head, unable to pull together a more coherent thought. Though he'd told her not to explain, the question had been tearing at him since the moment Clarissa appeared in that courtyard.

Why?

His mind returned to the tourney, to the moment she'd given him her favor. He'd won that match and returned to hand the white slip of fabric back. His hastily uttered invitation could have been met with derision or shock. Instead, she smiled at him, the same shy smile of the young woman he'd met outside her hall years earlier.

And nodded.

If her acceptance had surprised him, Aidan had been even more shocked when she'd arrived at the agreed-upon place, alone. And though she had not remained long enough, those brief, stolen moments, and the ones they managed to arrange over the next few days, had convinced him that he had met the woman he would marry.

His parents had been in love, and though he'd never said as much to Graeme, being born the younger son had allowed him one clear advantage. Though his brother was expected to make a good match, one that would firm a clan alliance or beget a new one, *he* was free to choose a wife. And though it was absurd to imagine he'd fallen in love with Lady Clarissa in such a short time, he had been nearly knocked to the ground by her beauty and smile. By the way she seemed to defy all odds with Theffield as a father. She was his opposite in every way. Kind and compassionate, the epitome of grace and strength.

Quite literally knocked to the ground. She'd so distracted him during his match, he'd nearly found himself staring up at the sky, bested by an Englishman. Then, despite her father's watchful eye, they managed to meet every day of the tournament.

That fateful day, they had planned to meet again. He thought it odd Lady Clarissa did not appear to witness his match that morn as she had for each one before it. He'd looked for her in the stands, of course. But there were many events, and she could have been perusing the wares of the merchants who came from afar to set up stands in the makeshift marketplace.

He'd felt like an untried lad that day, certainly not a man of five and twenty. Each moment he waited for her, his anticipation grew. Until it began to turn to dread.

Because she never came.

Never sent word, neither at the tournament nor any time afterward. He had learned by chance, nearly a year later, that she was married. He and Graeme had stopped at The Wild Boar, the only inn that managed to thrive despite the increasing tension along the border, and he'd heard her name mentioned above the din in the common room. At first, Aidan assumed he'd imagined it. But the black eye he received later that eve was anything but imagined. After defending her honor to a pair of Englishmen who thought it amusing to discuss Lord Stanley's quest for an heir in detail, Aidan was dragged from the inn by his brother.

Hell.

He didn't know what to think now. There were still so many unanswered questions.

"Were you betrothed when we met?"

The way she stiffened beneath his arms told him she had not fallen back asleep.

"No."

When she turned to face him, he instinctively tightened his grip to hold her more securely.

"When we returned home, he told me I'd be married immediately. He did not care that I'd met someone else. He did not even care to learn your name."

Softening toward her despite himself—his anger had been his only shield, and a faulty one at that—Aidan turned away. But he found himself glancing at her again as she blinked at him, expecting a response.

She was telling the truth.

In the short time he'd known her, Aidan had learned much about the only daughter of the Earl of Theffield. He'd been most impressed with her sentimentality and idealism, despite the treatment she'd received from the man who was supposed to love and protect her. Theffield had done neither of those things, but he had somehow managed to raise an extraordinary daughter. Though they had spent barely a sennight together, he'd learned his first instincts had been correct. Amidst turbulence and turmoil, divided allegiances and endless battles, Clarissa represented all that was good in the world.

She was good. Her heart, pure.

"How did you come to be here?"

When she pulled her bottom lip into her mouth, Aidan tried not to notice. Or stare.

Tried, and failed.

"As I said, Stanley appealed for our marriage to be annulled—"

"Why would he do such a thing?"

Again, that damn lip.

"I would prefer not to discuss it."

No matter, he could guess the reason. Stanley had married Clarissa for one reason alone, and if Aidan's suspicions were correct, the old man could take wife after wife and still fail to beget an heir.

"You misunderstand." He needed to soften his tone. It was certainly not her fault he was plagued by visions of the aging lord in a bed with her. "How did you come to be here, or back at Theffield? And why do we travel now to Sutworth?"

He had vowed not to ask questions. To provide the lady escort, drop her off, and then be gone. Now, it seemed he couldn't stop the questions from coming.

She met his eyes with a bravado he could tell she did not feel.

"When he received word that the annulment would be granted . . ."

She turned then, giving him her back. It was an infinitely less interesting view, if one did not account for silky locks that his hands ached to touch now that her hood was down . . .

The pain she'd endured was evident. He could feel the anger seeping from him, little by little, if indeed any remained at all.

How could I have been so foolish?

"My husband bade me leave."

She spoke the words so quietly he had to ask her to repeat them. When she did, a white-hot fury consumed him as he thought of Clarissa being sent away, without preamble, back to the man who had resigned her to such a fate in the first place.

Aidan was almost afraid to ask.

"Sutworth?"

Silence.

"Clarissa," he said as the very manor in question came into view ahead. "What do you plan to do at Sutworth Manor? And how did your father react—"

"He does not know."

Of course . . . she'd not told him about the annulment. But he would find out soon enough.

"What are you planning?"

He watched as her shoulders rose and fell.

"Clarissa—"

"I plan to ask Sutworth's priest to make contact with the nuns at Dunburg. I hope to join their order."

Aidan's heart skipped a beat and then threatened to lurch right out of his chest. Clarissa was going to become a nun?

The hell she was.

CHAPTER 7

"*W*ait! What are you doing?"

Distracted by their conversation, Clarissa had only just realized how close they'd come to the outer gatehouse of Sutworth Manor. If the guards saw Aidan . . .

"Escorting you to—"

"But you cannot be seen." Clarissa whipped around, taken aback by how handsome he was up close. His hair curled in so many places, including on his forehead. As the sky began to lighten, so too did his eyes, which appeared more green than brown in the light of morning.

"I will not leave you here—"

"You will."

On this, Clarissa refused to be dissuaded. She began to push against him to show the stubborn Scot just how serious she was.

"Do you mean to jump and break your neck?"

"Aye," she said, her voice firm. "I will do just that if you do not let me—"

"Clarissa," he warned, "stop or you will—"

"Break my neck, aye. I know."

When he finally slowed their mount, Clarissa nodded in

satisfaction. Unable to look away, knowing this would be the last time she would see him, she said, "Thank you for your escort—"

He rolled his eyes.

"Why do you mock me?" she asked.

Aidan ignored her and turned to his men. "Meet me at the river."

When he pulled his arms away from her, Clarissa mourned the loss of his heat. And before she realized what he was about, Aidan had also dismounted and was reaching for her. Lifting her as if she were no heavier than a sack of grain, he placed her back on the ground.

As he untied her belongings, Clarissa tested out the use of her legs, which were admittedly more than a bit wobbly. Her backside was so sore she cringed at the thought of sitting. And yet, all her thoughts were for him.

"Where are you going?" she asked.

Though it was obvious he meant to accompany her on foot, Clarissa refused to follow.

"My father cannot know you helped me here. If you are spotted—"

"I won't be."

He sounded so confident, as if he knew something she did not. Reluctantly, she began to follow him, the gatehouse, and its guards, looming ever closer.

"Aidan, this is far enough," she pressed.

He stopped and leveled a look at her that nearly made her laugh. It was patient and charming, a classic Aidan de Sowlis look. This was the same man who'd refused to leave her side those many years ago when he'd visited Theffield with his brother and father. The one who had covered for her when she thought to run away, an action that would have likely seen her beaten. Or, if she'd been successful, killed.

The time she fell half in love with him. Only half because she had been too young to understand what it meant to love. That had come later.

"I am aware, my lady, of what your father's knowledge of this particular adventure would do to our negotiations."

"Aidan, wait."

When he stopped, she considered her next words carefully. Just because she'd lost all hope didn't mean everyone around her should do the same. But she owed him the truth.

"I told you, and meant it. I know my father. He will not be convinced to help."

"He must help us. There is no other way."

So it was worse than she'd imagined as she sat inside the walls of her new prison these past two years. She'd heard, of course, of the deteriorating conditions along the border, but to have it confirmed . . . with the thought of her father as their only hope.

She sighed, not wanting to say any more. It would do no good.

"Come," he said, walking once more. "I know this area well."

Indeed, he did. At Aidan's direction, they'd skirted Sutworth's small village on their way here, and now Aidan led her down a path she had never seen before.

"If you continue walking along this path, it will lead you directly behind the northwest tower and dovecote. And there is little chance anyone other than Sutworth's men will see you."

Unlike the other road, this one was well hidden among the trees. And since Sutworth Manor was protected on three sides by cliffs rising from the deep gorge of the River Craig, Aidan was correct. It was nigh impossible she would be accosted.

Meeting her eyes, he added, "I will not leave the area until I see movement atop the gatehouse and know you are safe." With that, he handed her the satchel and bowed ever so slightly. "I am sorry, my lady."

Though what he was sorry for, Clarissa feared she'd never know. Because as quickly as he'd pulled her atop his horse back at

58

Theffield Castle, he was gone. Everything else she'd meant to tell him was to be left unsaid.

Turning toward the manor house, named as such only for its size and not its grandeur or, thankfully, its fortifications, Clarissa walked toward it. She'd only met the people who worked and lived here a handful of times in her life. Even so, it was easier to imagine the reception she might receive, or even the possibility they would send directly for her father, than it was to think about what she just had lost.

Again.

"You've TOLD me what he said." Graeme leaned back in his chair in his solar. "Now tell me what you think."

Aidan was about to explain to his brother that Theffield would likely help them, but Clarissa's words from that morning came back to him. She'd been adamant that her father would not aid their cause. But rather than ruminate on that fact, he'd spent his ride back to Highgate End thinking about the man's daughter instead. No matter how hard he tried, Aidan could not get her out of his head.

Lady Clarissa of Theffield.

A nun.

He shook his head. Never had there been a maid so ill-suited for that particular calling. Not, he chided himself, that a nun could not look as she did. Or have a body made for a man's hands. But that day by the lake, he had not been alone in his awareness of her, of how the air between them crackled with intensity.

He was not alone in his desire, and judging from the past day, that fact had not changed. Though of course, everything else *had* changed.

"I'm unsure," he said finally. "I believe his desire to host the most important event along the border will be our own salvation."

"And yet?"

His brother knew him well. As it was nearly midday, a meal awaited them in the great hall. When he was hungry, Graeme did not like to waste time with words.

"His daughter does not agree."

He'd considered not telling Graeme about her, and from his brother's expression, perhaps his first instinct—to stay quiet—had been correct. But he'd not kept anything from him before, and he would not do so now.

"Explain."

Shite.

"Just as we were leaving Theffield Castle, his daughter . . ."

Graeme raised his brows, no doubt thinking about Aidan's account of what had happened between them two years earlier.

"His daughter sought our help. She needed escort to Sutworth—"

"So why did her father not provide her escort? And what was she doing at—"

"Her father did not know she planned to hide away at Sutworth to convince their priest to sponsor her into the Benedictine Order of nuns at Dunburg."

If the situation were not so dire, he'd have laughed at Graeme's expression. "Theffield does not yet know Lord Stanley appealed for, and was granted, the right to annul their marriage."

Graeme looked every bit as shocked as Aidan had felt upon hearing Clarissa's plan. He waited as the information penetrated . . . and for the yelling that was sure to—

"You abducted the Earl of Theffield's daughter, the same earl who is our only chance at regaining any semblance of peace along the border . . ."

It seemed Graeme was too overwrought to continue. His anger was warranted. He should not have done this to him, to their clan, and yet he'd had no other choice.

His brother's fit of anger was interrupted by Gillian, who had come running into the room at the sound of shouting.

"What in the name of . . ."

She looked at Graeme first and then him. The sight of her, and her rounded belly, reminded him of the stakes. Of the danger he'd put them in.

"I'm sorry," he said. "I never should have agreed."

"Never should have agreed to what?" Gillian asked in confusion.

By now Graeme was standing . . . nay, pacing . . . and he continued to do so as Aidan explained the situation to Gillian. Her eyes seemed to widen with every word. When he finished, she said, "This does not seem like you, Aidan. But I can see you were just attempting to do the honorable thing for a woman in need—"

Aidan said, "If it were any other woman—"

"But it was not any other woman," Graeme said, his voice calmer now. "'Tis done."

"You never finished your story about the daughter," Gillian interjected. "You said you saw her again, years later. But you didn't tell me where, or what happened."

Graeme expelled a long, exaggerated breath. "They met again two years ago at the Tournament of the North. They recognized each other, and he gave the lady his favor before a joust. Somehow, despite the watchful eye of her very controlling father, the two managed a series of private meetings. But she failed to meet him at their final arranged rendezvous, and he never heard from her again."

And now his brother was not the only angry one in the room.

"You risked the mission for a woman who broke your heart—"

"She did not," he ground out, "break my heart."

"Ha!" Graeme scoffed. "Brother, you may have fooled yourself into believing as much, but you will never fool those who know you well." He turned back to Gillian. "I've never seen Aidan that way before. Until much later when we learned she had married. And then, he was worse."

"Married?" Gillian's hands flew to her mouth.

"Enough," Aidan bellowed. "That is enough."

He strode to the door and was about to leave when Graeme's voice stopped him.

"I assume no one knows you gave the lady escort?" He asked as chief, and not as his brother.

"None but the lady herself," he said without turning around. "As well as Lawrence and the other men."

"And you trust her to keep quiet?"

Did Aidan trust the woman he'd spent two years cursing? The one he'd thought, for the briefest of moments, he would make his wife?

"Aye, I do."

CHAPTER 8

*S*he should be happy.

In fact, Clarissa should be elated. For once, everything had fallen into place. Not only had she miraculously found an escort to Sutworth, but upon her arrival, she'd been treated better than she ever had in her life. Word of her presence had spread quickly, and she'd been given a joyous welcome. If they were surprised she'd arrived alone, none of them treated her as such. Rather, Clarissa had been fed and then shown to the beautiful chamber where she now sat.

Best of all, Father Patrick had agreed to help her.

She'd sought him out yesterday afternoon and asked to speak with him privately. Clarissa had always liked the portly man who smiled at everyone. Something about him had assured her that he would help, but even so, she'd woken up this morning expecting to find her world crashing down around her. Would her father somehow know where she'd gone? Would Father Patrick betray her confidence and send word to Theffield that his errant daughter was in hiding here at Sutworth? Instead, the priest had sought her out after morning mass with the happy news that all was being prepared.

He'd sent a missive to Dunburg Abbey requesting an audience. It was a formality, he assured her. The nuns would not turn away badly needed gold, nor a nobly born woman prepared to take her vows. In a few days' time, he would accompany her to Dunburg, where she would live out the remainder of her days.

"You can remain there, under their protection, until the annulment is official," he'd said. As to how they would know it had been made official, how long such a thing would take, and more importantly, if her father could arrive and drag her back to Theffield in the meantime . . . she still had many questions. Father Patrick admitted he did not have all of the answers, but once the nuns accepted her, he'd told her, she would indeed be safe, even from her father's meddling. He could not forcibly remove her from Dunburg without serious repercussions.

All had gone remarkably well, and yet . . .

Aidan.

She'd never thought to see him again.

Even though he'd changed, those changes had all been on the surface. The bedrock of Aidan de Sowlis was still very much intact. Clarissa closed her eyes, attempting to clear her mind of memories it would not serve her well to dwell upon. Aidan de Sowlis was part of her past, not her future.

"My lady, may I come in?"

"Of course." She nodded, waving her hand to indicate the maidservant was welcome. When she entered, Clarissa nearly gasped. The woman's hair was a remarkable mass of bright red curls.

"I was told you may need assistance?"

Clarissa realized she was being quite rude. Jumping from the bed, she greeted the newcomer.

"Aye, thank you. What is your name?"

"Kirstine, my lady."

She was perhaps ten and nine, and obviously new to Sutworth.

Though Clarissa had not visited for some years, no one who looked like the maid would have escaped her notice.

"You're not from here, are you?"

Kirstine's capable hands did not pause. She removed the items of clothing from Clarissa's bag and shook them out, one by one.

"Nay, my lady. I was born and raised in Barrington. When both of my parents died, I found work at the Anvil Inn. Master McConnell bade me come here, and I've been serving Sutworth since the last harvest."

McConnell was Sutworth's steward. Though her father did not care for the man, Clarissa liked him immensely.

"I'm sorry to hear of your parents," she said, taking advantage of the lilac-scented water Kirstine had brought. Dipping a small white cloth into the bowl, she began by washing her face and then moved to her neck.

"Thank you, my lady."

"Tell me of Sutworth. My father does not deign to visit often, so my knowledge of this magnificent place is sorely lacking."

Kirstine cocked her head to the side. "When were you here last?"

Clarissa tried to remember, but the days ran together, each more miserable than the last. With the exception of the tournament, and her journey here, so few of them had been filled with joy that Clarissa had stopped paying attention to the passing of time.

"Many years go," she said vaguely. "But I am glad to be here now."

When Kirstine looked at her this time, it was as if the other woman could see through her. It was not an unkindly gaze, but it made her feel uncomfortable nonetheless.

"Yet you are not staying."

Clarissa froze. The maid knew something.

"What do you—"

"I am sorry, my lady," she rushed to answer. "I'd been ordered to clean Father's chamber, and when you entered . . . I did not know what to do. I did not mean to listen, but you began speaking and . . ."

The maid hung her head.

"You were there. You heard everything."

It was not a question. Clarissa could feel her own heart pounding inside her chest. If word spread of her true intentions . . .

"I am so sorry, my lady. As I said, I did not mean—"

It struck Clarissa that the woman likely feared for her position. Clarissa's father was notoriously unforgiving of the smallest errors in judgment.

"Shhh," she said, willing the maid to look at her. She crossed the room and placed a hand on Kirstine's shoulder. "I understand."

The woman's tear-filled eyes confirmed her suspicion. Her father, who rarely came to Sutworth Manor, had sufficiently terrified the staff.

"I am not my father," she said simply.

Kirstine seemed to understand. She swallowed. "I am so very—"

"Sorry, I know." Clarissa removed her hand. "Please . . . please do not tell anyone of my plans. If the wrong person learns of them—"

"You fear him too?"

Clarissa did not have to ask of whom she spoke.

"Aye."

Kirstine wiped her eyes with her thumb. "I've never even met the man."

Clarissa hoped she never would. "So you can understand my need to keep my intentions a secret?"

Kirstine nodded. "But do you truly believe this is the only way? You are prepared to give your life to God?"

Prepared? Nay. No nun should react to a man with the fluttering sense of anticipation she felt toward Aidan. But she had no other choice. Clarissa refused to be married to another man like Lord Stanley.

"There is no other way."

Kirstine frowned, evidently agreeing. "It just seems wrong for a woman as beautiful as you . . ."

If she were beautiful, then Kirstine was positively ravishing. But it did not matter what either of them looked like. If anything, beauty was a curse in this world, one dominated by power and strength. It hardly mattered that she was the daughter of an earl. She and Kirstine were similar in more ways than they were not. And like the maid, Clarissa would do what she must to survive.

"AIDAN, ARE YOU LISTENING?"

In truth, he was not. Something about another attack, further west.

"I heard some. What were you saying?"

Graeme crossed his arms and waited. He supposed his brother wished for him to explain what distracted him, though he'd likely not care for the answer.

Telling his brother *I was thinking of the very lady who has the ability to unravel all of our plans; in fact, I was considering going to Sutworth Manor, just to ensure she is well* would not do. Nay, he would keep those thoughts to himself.

"Douglas is becoming impatient. He sent word this morning that unless Theffield capitulates soon, he'll not be able to persuade the clans to our cause," Graeme repeated.

Aidan stood. The midday meal had ended, and he no longer wished to sit still.

Clarissa had been at Sutworth Manor for a full day now. How had the priest reacted to her plan? Would he help her? Or betray her to her father?

"Aidan!"

His reverie was broken by his sister-in-law's shriek from the hall entrance. Allie, with her husband. The streaks of dark blond in Allie's brown hair were not unlike the streak of wildness she possessed, the most noticeable difference between her and Gillian, who was currently resting in her bedchamber. The visit was unexpected, but no less welcome. He quite missed Allie, and the longsword lessons he'd given her while she lived at Highgate End.

Both he and Graeme left the trestle table to greet them, Aidan's hand falling to the dirk that never left his side. Given to him by Allie's husband, Reid, the youngest of the four Kerr brothers, it reminded him of the role he'd played in bringing the couple together. A role he was quite proud of, but one which had nearly cost him Gillian's loyalty.

She'd not cared for Reid. Hated him, in fact. But luckily, those sentiments were firmly in the past. As they reached the newcomers, Aidan shook Reid's hand. Or attempted to at least. Allie threw her arms around him, nearly stumbling in her eagerness, as everyone around them laughed.

"'Tis been too long," she said, letting go.

Her smile was as radiant as ever, the happiness she enjoyed with her new husband evident. "Not so long, sister."

Then his eye caught Reid's, and he knew this was no simple familial visit. They came bearing news, and the way things were going lately, the tidings would not be welcome.

"She insisted on accompanying me."

Allie shrugged. "He insisted on making it difficult."

Aidan listened to their banter with pride, happy to have been right about them from the start. They were good for each other. They were happy together. Would he and Clarissa have ever achieved this easiness with each other?

And then Allie leveled a look of her own at him.

Uh-oh.

He knew that look. She'd noticed his expression.

"Will you walk with me?" she asked.

As if he had a choice. She would not be waylaid, and if her expression were any indication, this would not be an entirely comfortable discussion.

"I will share Reid's news but have some of my own," Allie added.

"Of course," he said, following her from the hall into the courtyard. Ignoring the activity around them, the squeals of young children running past and the distant sounds of the armory, Aidan and Allie walked up a stone stairwell that led to an eastern-facing wall-walk. It was only when they arrived at the top, as he laid a hand on the stone in front of them and looked up at the cloudless sky, that Allie began her assault.

"Tell me," she said simply.

He pretended to misunderstand.

"It seems there has been another attack—"

"*Aidan.*"

His connection to Allie had been this way from the start. They were able to read each other's signals as if they'd been raised brother and sister in truth. He could try to pretend all was well, but she would learn of Clarissa from Gillian anyway. Strangely relieved to talk to someone about this nagging feeling that he'd abandoned Clarissa, he told her everything.

From their first meeting at Theffield Castle to their unexpected reunion. He told her that he felt poorly for leaving Clarissa in front of Sutworth Manor, alone and with an uncertain future, but even more poorly for putting his clan in danger. When he was finished, Aidan did not know what to expect. Which was typical when dealing with Allie.

"Why are you here?" she blurted finally.

"Pardon?"

"Here. At Highgate. Why are you here and not there?"

She was surely jesting. "Did you not hear me? She is Theffield's daughter. And in hiding from her own father. When he finds out—"

Allie's eyes narrowed. "He will do what, precisely? Come to Sutworth to fetch her? If she's lucky, the lady will already be gone, her life given to God. If not, what do you suppose he will do?"

He refused to answer that particular question.

"Allie, if I were to aid her further and Theffield learned of my interference—"

"Then ensure he does not."

Late last eve, after everyone else was abed, he'd thought of just that. Aidan knew how to breach the castle walls. But if he were discovered . . .

"If I'm found sneaking into Sutworth, my guilt will be undeniable. And even if the men are not loyal to him—"

"Then do not sneak. Simply pay her a visit."

Allie was even madder than he'd thought. "Why did I not think of that? Simply ride to Sutworth, announce myself, and walk straightway into the hall asking for Lady Clarissa. 'Tis a fine plan—"

"For someone who was quite clever in helping me find a way to be with Reid, you're acting oafish. Of course you will not ask for her. Simply a friendly visit from a neighbor—"

"Who has not been to Sutworth in some years."

"But do they not warrant a warning too? The same warning about the current troubles that Reid and I came here to deliver?"

She'd managed to surprise him. He'd almost forgotten they had another purpose in being here. "What warning?"

Allie swallowed. "The Waryns are worried. Apparently the unrest has spread to the east. Even the most moderate English border lords are beginning to call to arms."

It was what they feared would happen if the Day of Truce fell apart permanently. With the English king's health deteriorating, and his heir overseas on Crusade, the borders apparently did not warrant the attention of those in power.

"Another reason not to incite trouble with the only man who may help us avoid war."

"And that is the only reason you won't go to Sutworth?"

Nay, not the only reason at all. But Aidan was finished with this conversation.

"You and Gillian are safe, for the moment. Our clan is safe. Nothing else—"

"Matters, I know. You've done everything possible to ensure it is so."

Aidan straightened, knowing that was not true. Escorting Clarissa had put them in jeopardy.

"You do not understand—"

"Oh, aye, I understand well," Allie said. "It is you who does not understand. But you will."

With that cryptic statement, she walked away.

Laughing aloud, not caring if the guards overheard him and thought him daft, Aidan could not help but appreciate the situation. Allie was urging him to steal away to Sutworth—just like he'd helped her steal away to Brockburg when she and Reid were separated.

But this was different. Gillian had disliked her sister's choice, aye, but that was not the same as risking the wrath of the Earl of Theffield. Yet . . . if Clarissa did not tell anyone how she'd come to be at Sutworth, was there really any danger in paying her a visit as Allie had suggested?

Do not attempt to fool yourself. Of course there is a danger.

But his sister-in-law was right on one account. He could not sit here and wait to learn of Clarissa's fate. He would leave a quick message to Graeme, and then he would go to Sutworth and return before nightfall.

Just to ensure all was well.

CHAPTER 9

Though not as large as Theffield Castle, Sutworth Manor was every bit as opulent. Clarissa spied her father's hand in small details throughout the hall. Overly bright tapestries chronicling the exploits of English kings lined the walls. He'd certainly done nothing to endear himself to the people here, proud borderers who likely did not appreciate the flaunting of their very English lord. Though it was fairly common for nobles on both sides of the border to own estates in both England and Scotland, she suspected most of them attempted to assimilate a bit more than her father had.

Of course they hated him here. And, unlike at Theffield, the servants were not as circumspect in their disrespect of their master. When she entered the hall for the midday meal, Clarissa did not know what to expect. But it didn't take long to realize the very thing she feared most had happened.

They knew why she was here.

First, the steward had approached her with a whispered apology. "I'm sorry, my lady. We will protect your secret." Someone, likely Father Patrick, had told him the truth.

So much for the man's vow of secrecy.

Then, as the meal was served, another servant gave her a pitying glance and sad smile. The servants' behavior was pronounced enough that she left the head table in search of Kirstine.

The maid confirmed what she already knew—they were all aware of her situation—and promised it was not her who told. Word had already spread throughout the manor. She vowed to learn what she could and report back to Clarissa at the head table.

Fulfilling her promise, Kirstine returned with news a short time later as Clarissa ate a bowl of rather tasty stew alone at the head table. Those retainers who also ate in the hall hardly seemed to notice her.

"Father Patrick told the steward of your plight. And it seems the news spread from there."

Clarissa's heart sank.

"But do not fret, my lady!" The maid lowered her voice. "There is no great love here for your father, begging my pardon, and all of us are willing to help. In fact, we are most anxious to do so."

That was all well until the wrong person learned of her true purpose here. But her troubles were hers alone, not the maid's.

"Thank you, Kirstine."

Dismissing her, Clarissa decided she was no longer hungry. She left the high table in a hurry, which was how she came to nearly collide with . . .

"Oh!"

She stopped just short of her guest and Master Gavin, who had apparently entered together from the double door of the small keep. Sutworth Manor had been built in stages, the small keep ironically the name for the largest of three towers connected by shouldered archways.

"My lady." Aidan bowed as grandly as any gentleman. "You are Lord Theffield's daughter, are you not?"

Gavin appeared confused by the hurried greeting. By rights, the steward should have introduced them, but Aidan had needed to convey a message. She understood immediately and replied in kind.

"I am," she said. "Though it appears you do not remember our last meeting."

Aidan's eyes widened.

"You visited Theffield with your brother and father many years ago. Through God's grace, you've not changed much."

When he smiled, a genuine smile that did not make her feel as if she'd done something wrong, Clarissa's knees weakened, though thankfully they continued to support her.

"What brings you to Sutworth?"

She could tell Gavin wanted to break protocol and stay for the conversation—and she suspected he would not go far when he nodded in parting and walked away.

"I came to speak to whomever is in charge here about the current troubles along the border. Had I known you were in residence, I would have come to speak to you, or your father, sooner."

Clarissa began walking, leading them out of the corridor and toward the door from which he'd entered the hall. They needed to find somewhere more private. A challenge inside a manor house such as Sutworth.

"I regret to inform you that my father is not here," she said, although nothing was less regrettable than that fact. "I am here alone," she continued as they stopped in front of the wooden doors. Divided by a thin line of stone, the two doors stood side by side as if standing guard. Pushing the iron handle of the one on the right, Aidan led her into the small inner courtyard. Sutworth Manor had a much more compact design than Theffield. The manor house, inner courtyard, and outer courtyard were arranged in a straight line courtesy of the cliffs on three sides.

Though much of the manor's activity occurred in the larger outer courtyard, Clarissa still did not yet feel safe from watchful eyes. She led him to an unusual feature she'd once inquired about as a young girl, the caponier. Though the roofed passageway had been built as an added fortification inside the ditch between the inner and outer walls, it had quickly been abandoned.

The guards stationed above them were sure to notice that she and Aidan had entered the caponier alone. But she would worry about that later, if necessary.

They did not speak again until they entered the abandoned passageway. The exit had been filled in with stone long ago, and the only light flowed in from the entrance above them.

"What are you doing here?" she finally asked.

She was sure her voice betrayed her.

Clarissa had never expected to see him again.

"I had to know you were safe." His deep voice echoed against the cold stone walls. "Are you? Safe?"

"I don't know."

Clarissa explained what had happened since her arrival, still unable to believe he was at Sutworth. "But what of you? What if my father learns of your visit?"

Aidan shrugged. "Perhaps he will be grateful that Clan Scott is an ally to the people of Sutworth at such a time. I came, after all, to relay news from across the border." He looked directly into her eyes. "Not to see you."

Clarissa swallowed. "Of course."

None knew of his escort. But his visit was still risky.

"Thank you for your concern—"

"I loved you, Clarissa."

The words pierced her heart. Nothing he could have said would have surprised her more. She didn't know how to respond.

Loved. Of course he did not love her still. Why would he? She'd betrayed him in the very worst way.

"I should not have come—"

She reached out without thinking as Aidan turned to leave. His hand in hers reminded her of their contact as they rode to Sutworth. Now, as then, it was much more than a simple touch. Heat shot through his hand to hers, pooling in her very core. She tried to block out the memory that refused to be denied. Clarissa remembered their kiss well. Remembered how it had made her feel.

"Do not go."

She had no right to ask him to stay. It endangered them both. And yet, the thought of seeing him walk away again . . .

He did not pull his hand from her grasp. Instead, he parted his fingers until her own slipped into the cracks between them. When he closed them again, their hands entwined, Clarissa could hardly breathe.

Something had changed between them.

Had he forgiven her for leaving that day? Why else would he have returned? And why did he have to be so handsome? The light stubble along his cheek and jaw had grown in just a bit more, and Clarissa wanted desperately to feel it against her own cheek.

She wanted him to kiss her again.

"I am still married," she blurted, his slow smile making her wish she'd not opened her mouth.

"I am aware."

Aidan did not move toward her. Instead, he stood there, so close she could smell him rather than the stale air around them. She could see the rise and fall of his chest beneath his simple linen tunic. He was so much larger than her, yet so very, very gentle.

"I would see you again."

The statement seemed to surprise him as much as it did her.

"I do not know how long it will take for the nuns to reply. Or if someone here will betray me to my father first."

Loved, she reminded herself.

That sentiment was firmly in the past for him, and she'd do well to remember it. For Clarissa, it was not, nor had it ever been. She'd fallen in love with Aidan de Sowlis at that tournament, perhaps even before that when she was a young girl. If she'd ever doubted that truth, it was impossible to deny it any longer. She wanted nothing more than to stay in this caponier, enjoying the warmth and strength of his firm grip, sheltered from the world above.

But it could not be so.

"You are not the woman I stood next to at that lake, are you?"

"Nay, I am not. Lord Stanley has ensured that naïve young woman is gone forever."

The old Clarissa may have blurted something silly, like "Take me with you" or "Maybe there is a way for us." But she'd learned from her mistakes.

"I would like nothing more than to see you again," she said. "But it will not make it any easier for me to leave."

Aidan opened his mouth to say something, but she would never know what. He closed it, waited a moment, and then asked, "Will you send word when you arrive safely at Dunburg Abbey?"

She wanted to tell him that she'd not be going. That she could never give herself to God when she was still in love with *him*. That the thoughts she had of him late, late at night, alone in her bed, were anything but pure. That she was sorry for foolishly trusting her father at the tournament.

Instead, she said, "Aye."

And when he released his hand from hers, she did not seek it out again. Nor did she go after him when Aidan turned to walk back up the stairs. Instead, she stood there, staring at the pinprick of light, waiting . . . for what? He was gone. She'd told him to leave. Because she had no other choice.

Or did she?

AIDAN THANKED the groom and was about to lead his horse outside when she stopped him.

"Would you . . ."

He turned and stared. Clarissa looked the same as she had moments before—the fitted bodice of her deep blue gown leaving little question of what lay beneath . . . her hair pulled back on the sides but otherwise completely free of any adornments.

But somehow she looked different too.

"Would you care to stay for the meal?"

Since supper would not be for some time, Clarissa was not merely being polite. She was asking him to stay the day, and though he knew he should not . . . he'd been both disappointed and relieved when she'd pushed him away . . . Aidan was powerless to refuse the invitation he'd hoped to receive.

"Aye," he said, handing the reins back to the confused groom. And then, for the boy's benefit, "It will provide me with the opportunity to speak further with your marshal."

In fact, he'd already spoken to Sutworth's marshal, and had no further news for the man who would attempt to keep Sutworth safe during these troubled times.

"Very good." She gestured to the front of the stable. "Shall we?"

Following her back outside, Aidan thought of Graeme. By now his brother would know he'd come here. If he were being honest, he'd not have an easy time refuting Graeme's arguments for why he should have instead stayed home. Despite Allie's encouragement, he knew it had been a bad decision, and staying was a worse one yet.

But the pull he felt toward Clarissa was stronger than his good sense. She was so damn lovely. Aidan wished to wrap his hands around her father's neck at the thought of what he'd done to them. To her . . .

"We should stay away from the keep," she said, guiding him to a familiar path. "To the secret pathway where you brought me yesterday?"

They'd ventured through the inner and outer courtyard and to the other side of the great gatehouse. Just to the left of the main road leading directly to the entrance of the estate, not far from the top of the eastern cliff, a break in the tree line announced a footpath.

"Graeme and I explored it once, years ago. Neither you nor your father were here. I believe it was the last time I'd visited Sutworth until now."

Without speaking of their destination, they walked toward the path.

"You've not been back since?"

"Nay. Your father made it clear Sutworth was his in name only. It's lucky, I think, Sutworth has not yet been attacked since the lack of leadership here is well known along the border."

They continued down the trail, which reminded him . . .

"You will be questioned about my visit. Coming here, alone, will not help your cause," he said.

Clarissa seemed to consider that for a moment before she answered him. "There are already so many questions. My arrival, my plans—"

"To join the nuns at Dunburg?" Every part of him wanted to shout, *No!*

"Aye," she said, seemingly as disappointed about the prospect as he.

Aidan stopped. This had to be said. He'd not forgive himself if he kept quiet.

"You don't belong there."

Clarissa stopped alongside him, the corner of her lower lip curling inside, under her teeth.

"While I waited for you that day, before I realized you were not coming—"

"Aidan—"

"Nay, lass. I want you to know."

He looked up, the stab in his chest a very different one than when he'd thought of her these past two years.

"I tried to understand how a woman like you could have been raised by a man like him. I wondered if he'd accept me and thought of how lucky I was to have met you, again."

She abused her poor lip, though he'd very much like to be so abused.

"When you did not come, I wondered what I had said to offend you. And later, I wondered if you'd already known about your betrothal to Stanley. I should have guessed the truth."

He'd failed her then and was doing so now.

She released her lips and clasped her hands together in front of her. "Knowing you likely hated me was, is, difficult."

"I don't hate you, Clarissa. I could never hate you."

Neither of them spoke for a time. A gentle rustling of leaves and distant call from above was the only sound, with the exception of Clarissa's breathing. With every rise and fall of her chest, Aidan found himself questioning everything. He'd convinced himself that as long as his family was happy, and safe, nothing else mattered.

But something else did.

Clarissa had always mattered.

"My maid," she said, though Aidan wasn't sure where the thought had come from. "She is the kindest, gentlest woman in the world. It was she who convinced me that my father was wrong, that I did not kill my mother, and yet—"

"How could you think such a thing?"

He knew the answer as soon as he posed the question. *Of course* the man blamed her for her mother's death. He was a monster.

"Tell me what happened, Clarissa," he said in a softer tone.

The slight shrug of her shoulders undermined the devastation on her face.

"As I said, I made a mistake. I thought for one brief moment that maybe he would soften toward me. That he'd allowed me to attend the tournament because he was ready to show me the wider world . . . so I told him. It was the biggest mistake of my life. I saw myself married so quickly neither I nor Eda could prepare, not that there was anything I could have done, really."

He knew all of that already. "And the marriage?"

Clarissa opened her mouth, but no sound emerged. She promptly closed it again. "Was possibly better than living with my father. Except . . ."

God, he would kill them. Both. If her husband had abused her . . .

"Did he hurt you?"

She frowned. "I suppose not—"

"Suppose?"

"Nay, not really." The light pinks spots on her cheeks told him to stop questioning her, though he found himself thinking about what those Englishmen had spoken of at The Wild Boar. Of foul Stanley's quest for an heir.

"I am so sorry, Clarissa."

He had no words to explain how sorry he was for having failed her.

"'Tis not your fault that my father—"

"'Tis my fault for assuming the worst. I had means to contact you, but I did not. Instead I abandoned you to—"

"'Tis I who abandoned you."

Foolishly, he reached for her hand again. When she did not protest, he took them both in his. That same jolt of heat surged through him.

"You cannot do this."

But he could see in her eyes that she would.

"I have no choice."

Stay with me.

He wanted to say the words so badly, but he squeezed her hands instead. Aidan didn't know which was stronger, the urge to take her in his arms or the urge to put her back on his horse and ride straight to Highgate End.

In the end, he did neither.

"I wish I could disagree with you."

Her rueful smile told Aidan what he already knew. She could

not come with him. Absconding with Theffield's daughter would make an enemy of him. He would refuse to deal with Caxton, and chaos would surely follow.

"Delay it," he found himself saying. "Once your father agrees, and Caxton is replaced—"

"And if he does not agree?"

"Then we will no longer need him."

The look of determination on her face was one he knew well. He'd seen it before on his new sister Allie's face. She was going to say no.

"If I do not go to Dunburg Abbey, he will find me. When he does, I will have no recourse. And I will *not* marry again."

Not even to me?

"Then go to Dunburg if you must, but do not say your vows. Wait for me—"

"I cannot. Until I say them, I will be vulnerable. My father will still have a claim on me."

He wanted to scream. He wanted to punch Theffield in the throat. He wanted to disagree with her, but she had the right of it. Until she said the words—

"But you are still married! You cannot take the vows while you are wed. If he finds you before—"

"Father Patrick assured me the Benedictine Order allows for a postulant to still be married. Once the annulment is official, I will become a novice. Under the rule of the Church, I will be the property of God, not of my father."

He opened his mouth to object, but his gentle English lass squeezed his fingers once more and let them go.

"'Tis done."

As she began to walk back toward the keep, Aidan watched her walk away. He refused to accept such a fate for her. He had already lost her once.

But how could he hope to save both her *and* the borderlands?

CHAPTER 10

o one questioned his presence. In fact, everyone seemed as enthralled by Aidan as she was. After a tour of Sutworth, one she was hardly qualified to offer considering how infrequently she'd been here growing up, they stood upon the wall-walk of the southeast tower, looking out at the impressive view and talking. He did not move to hold her hand again, wise given they could be seen, if not heard, by at least one guard. But she almost wished he had done so anyway.

If not for the shadow cast by his impending leave-taking, this would have been the happiest day of her life. He laughed to learn how she'd gotten away from her father to meet him during the tournament, though it had been nothing more than her "using the time to pray," a practice with which he always approved. She smiled at his memory of their first encounter years before. He claimed to have been drawn to her then, and if she had not felt the same way, Clarissa may not have been inclined to believe him.

Rather than sit at the head table in the hall, on display in front of people she hardly knew, Clarissa asked for their evening meal to be brought to the solar. According to custom, the small, private room was located just off the master bedchamber on the second floor of the keep. Courtesy of its shuttered windows, which had been thrown open upon her arrival, it was one of the best-lit chambers in the manor. Both the solar and master chamber had been freshly scrubbed and prepared for her. She'd thought of asking for another chamber to sleep in instead, but apparently no one thought of the room as her father's.

But darkness had fallen, and after they finished their repast, it was time for him to leave. For a moment at the meal, she had put aside all but the ease with which they sat side by side, conversing.

"May I return again tomorrow?"

Clara held her breath when they stood. Aidan had come alone, and though he insisted he was quite safe on both Sutworth and Clan Scott land, she knew reivers preferred to ride by moonlight. Emboldened by the current political climate, they grew more active and aggressive each day.

I should say no.

"Aye. I would like that, but won't your brother be angry?"

They'd talked about what it meant, him being here, and she knew Aidan recognized the dangers. Evidently, his brother thought him foolish.

"He will."

His gaze, unwavering, did not make her feel uncomfortable. Just the opposite, in fact. She could not look away. She'd noticed his eyes turned more green when he looked at her this way.

Her pulse raced as the implication of his words penetrated. He should not be here and should definitely not return. But he would anyway.

And at that moment, Clarissa never wanted anything more than Aidan de Sowlis to lean over and kiss her. She'd thought of their kiss by the lake on so many lonely nights. Had memory served her well, or would it be disappointing? Somehow she doubted it.

"If you only knew how much I want it too," he said.

Oh dear! Clarissa had been caught staring at his lips. Rather than deny it, she met his eyes once again and said, "I've thought of it so many times. It was my first, and only, kiss."

His eyes narrowed. "Your husband?"

"Never touched me in that way."

Though he had poised himself above her, his white skin gleaming in the darkness of their chamber, he'd never kissed her. Never caressed her. She'd not wanted to look down, to look at him, but she had been unable to stop herself.

Clarissa shuddered at the memory.

"What did he do to you?"

She shook her head. "It doesn't matter."

He reached out so quickly she hardly had time to react. His hand splayed across her cheek, the soft caress of a lover. Clarissa closed her eyes at the touch, attempting to remember it so she could keep it with her forever.

"I would kiss you," he said. "If you were mine to kiss."

Her eyes flew open.

"And it would not be as chaste as the one we shared by the lake."

Chaste? What did he mean by that? The soft touch of his lips had been perfect, and every day they'd spent together she had wished to repeat it.

As Clarissa's lips parted, his thumb edged closer and closer to them until it rested on the very edge of her lower lip. When he ran his thumb across her lip, a pool of heat filled her very core. She wanted . . .

And then he dropped his hand away, stood back from her and closed his eyes.

"Aidan?"

That feeling . . . when he'd touched her . . .

"What are we doing?" he asked, his voice strained.

She didn't think he would appreciate "falling in love, again" for an answer. Or maybe she'd never stopped loving him.

"I don't know how long it will be until we receive word from Dunburg," she said instead. "And if my father learns of my whereabouts first . . ."

He likely did not even realize that his hand was shifting toward his side. When he was angry, Aidan's hand crept closer to the dirk that never left his hip. She'd noticed that as they rode here from Theffield—and he'd done the same thing today, whenever her father was mentioned.

"I will take whatever time is given to us."

Her shoulders sagged with relief. She'd feared for a moment he'd changed his mind. And though it might be easier to part from him now than it would be in a few days, Clarissa could not make herself say the words that would keep him away.

"Meet me on the secret path."

"It is not so secret to those who live here. How will you explain—"

"I will find a way. Tomorrow, after the sixth hour bell, I will be there."

"As will I," she said.

With a slight bow, Aidan was gone.

He strode out of the solar, leaving her standing there, staring after him. No good would come of their meeting again. They both knew it, but Clarissa was as powerless to tell Aidan to stay away as she'd been to stop her father from taking her home from that tournament.

The outcome would be another unhappy ending, but Clarissa no longer cared.

A SENNIGHT HAD PASSED since Aidan's initial visit to Sutworth Manor. Each day had been much the same. Meetings with Graeme and Reid, training with the men, and avoiding Gillian and Allie's questions about his midday rides. Graeme had not been pleased that first day, and he'd thought to avoid another unpleasant conversation by keeping subsequent visits quiet. They were all becoming suspicious, but while his brother avoided questioning him, his *sisters* had no such qualms. And so he'd dispensed excuses. One day, he'd claimed to visit Lawrence. Another, the village.

If he felt poorly about deceiving his brother, Aidan pushed those feelings aside. He was not jeopardizing their mission in any way. He'd not tossed Clarissa onto his horse and absconded to Highgate with her—a scenario that consumed his every waking thought—so he refused to feel poorly any longer for his actions.

Even though he knew he should.

So when Allie whispered "Meet me at the training yard" to him at supper, he understood why she wished to speak with him privately—to press him about Clarissa. After all, her skill with the longsword was no longer a secret, and the invitation harkened back to how things had been before, back when they'd kept her developing skill to themselves.

Stopping in the bakehouse first for a few chunks of bread—pried away with difficulty from the covetous baker—he made his way back down the hill and away from the keep, trying, unsuccessfully, not to think of *her*.

And yet his thoughts lingered on Clarissa's easy smile. Though she claimed not to be the same since Lord Stanley, he did not believe it fully. The goodness that had attracted him to her still shone through in every word, every smile. Better to think of that smile than the endearing way she bit her lip.

"Over here."

Though she was dressed for training, the new sword Reid had commissioned for her at her side, it was clear his impulse had been correct. Allie was here to talk and not to train.

"I've news for you."

Her smile was so infectious, he found himself smiling back.

This was not about his daily rides then, but Allie was undoubtedly up to something.

"You've a look about you, lass—"

"A look? Of which sort?"

He folded his arms. "Allie . . . ," he warned.

The stress of the last days had weighed on him. Aidan was not his playful self, and Allie must have sensed as much.

"I could not chance being overheard in the hall."

"What is this—"

"The annulment. It is done."

The look she gave him penetrated before her words did. Assured, confident and thoroughly pleased, Allie waited for his reaction. She could not mean—

"Did you hear me?"

"It would be difficult not to do so with you shouting at me."

He teased her often about her enthusiastic way of communicating, which was much more ardent than Gillian's method of delivery. In truth, he was still attempting to decipher her words.

"*The* annulment? Clarissa's annulment?"

"Nay, Aidan. The other one that promises to alter the course of your life."

He simply stared.

"Aye, Lady Clarissa's annulment! Who do you believe I—"

"How could you know about such a thing?"

He'd seen Clarissa just the day before, and she had not told him anything of the sort.

"Donnon, the sheepherder. You know, the one whose wife was killed by—"

"Aye, I know Donnon well." Aidan did not even attempt to hide his impatience.

"I was speaking with him earlier, and he heard from Ferguson MacDuff, who had just come from The Wild Boar, that Lord Stanley is already betrothed for the third time, now that his annulment to Lady Clarissa has been finalized. In fact, talk of it is rampant according to—"

"No."

It could not be. If what Allie said was true and Stanley's betrothal was already a well-known fact, it meant Clarissa's father had to know by now. "No . . . not already."

His stomach felt as hard as a rock, the sensation not nearly as unwelcome as Allie's news.

"I paid a visit to . . . Aidan, are you ill?"

He had to leave at once. "Do you know what this means?"

Allie smiled. "It means that you can go to her. Of course, you've been going to her each day, but now—"

"What did you say?"

No maid had ever looked more innocent.

"You said once that it feels as if you've known me since birth. Though your daily rides were most unusual, it took me some time to sort out. After all, you told me of that first visit, why not the subsequent ones."

"Allie!" He loved her, but Aidan also wanted to shake her at the moment. "Who else knows?"

She mimicked his earlier stance, crossing her arms in front of her. "You mean to ask, 'Does Graeme know?'" Allie pretended to consider the question. "Is it not odd that you once helped me overcome my sister's reluctance to accept Reid, and I am now doing the very same for you?"

Aidan's heart threatened to explode. "This is not simply a disagreement between siblings. Gillian was the only barrier that stood between you and Reid. In this situation, Graeme has every reason to be upset. My attachment to her could jeopardize everything. And you believe just because her marriage is no longer—"

"I've never seen you this way," she said, reaching out to touch his arm. The sympathy in her eyes sliced through him. "The people you love are happy. Do you not believe you also deserve—"

"It does not matter what I deserve. Clarissa and I . . . we cannot be."

"But once her father agrees to remove Caxton—"

"It will be too late. Besides which, Theffield could easily go back on his word." Hadn't he thought the situation through each and every night? Aidan pulled his arm away and shook his head. "This is no time to play matchmaker, Allie. It is simply not possible—"

"Then why do you see her each day?"

"It docs not matter why," he lashed out. "She cannot wait for the abbess any longer. If her father finds her—"

"Aidan . . ."

It was the gentle tone that kept him pinned to the spot.

"You love her."

Dear God, he did. He had never stopped loving her. And that was why he had to ensure she left for Dunburg. Now. "My feelings matter not."

"There must be a way for you to be together."

"I must go."

When Allie smiled once again, he realized she had misunderstood.

"I must go tell her to leave tonight. I will escort her to the abbey," he thought aloud.

Allie was incredulous. "Aidan, you cannot—"

"You don't understand the political situation," he said. "You and Clarissa were raised in much the same way. Sheltered, unaware of—"

"Do not insult me."

And now she was furious with him. But how else could he explain to her what would happen if he were caught with Clarissa? Each time he saw her, each time he helped her against Theffield's wishes, he further jeopardized the future of the Day of Truce. These past days with her . . . they had been the best of Aidan's life, but they both knew their time was limited.

"I'm sorry," he said, and meant it. "Tell Graeme everything," he added, aware his brother would not be pleased. But it no longer mattered. By the time he came back, Clarissa would be safely installed at Dunburg Abbey.

And if the nuns do not agree to take her?

They would. The jewels she brought them would ensure it. The question was not if they would take her, but how Aidan could bear to leave her there, never to see her again.

CHAPTER 11

*B*y the time they reached Sutworth, all was quiet. None but the guards stirred at this late hour, and though he and Lawrence had been admitted entry easily enough, they'd been provided with an escort to the keep. It was no less than he would expect. In fact, Aidan silently praised their caution, for even though the men here knew him, it was a most unusual hour for a social visit.

Having handed off their mounts to a sleepy stablehand, the small party walked toward the keep's entrance, their steps echoing loudly in the quiet courtyard. Dry dirt and small rocks crunched beneath their feet, testament to the unusually long stretch of days without rain.

Lawrence glanced at him as if to ask, yet again, what they were doing here. It had not taken Aidan long to realize it would be wise to have at least one man by his side. Already a distance from Highgate End, he'd quickly dismissed the idea of returning for his brother. The chief could not be seen here, even if he agreed to come.

A borderer his entire life, his friend had no love for the English. While Aidan's father had been a tolerant man, the same could not be said for the chief of Clan Karyn. As Lawrence had said often enough, "If the bastards had not routed out my family from their ancestral home, I may have been of a different opinion."

Hence his decision to seek Lawrence's help. Aidan knew he'd not pass up a chance to rattle their southern neighbors.

"What do you plan, de Sowlis?" he'd said. "To demand to see the lady abed? All of Sutworth is likely sleeping. Much like I was before you arrived."

Aidan had ignored his friend's mocking tone.

Of course, Lawrence had come anyway, thank God.

"My lords," the guard said as they arrived at the keep. Aidan had lifted his fist to knock when one of the large wooden doors swung open.

Expecting the steward, Aidan's eyes widened at the sight that greeted them.

Sucking in a breath, he took in the blue gown lined with a paler blue around the collar and sleeves, a vision of indescribable loveliness. But why was she here at the entrance of the manor, greeting him as if it were midday?

"I saw you approaching."

She did not explain further but instead stepped aside to allow them entrance.

"My lady," Lawrence said beside him, reminding Aidan of his friend's presence.

"Well met, even at such an hour," she greeted him back. And finally, though it had taken him a moment, Aidan found his voice.

"I must speak to you about an urgent matter."

Though the lone servant and guard had moved off, they were still listening. And likely prepared to wake their friends with the tale of two men appearing at such an hour, unannounced, asking to speak with their lady.

"What is so urgent to warrant such a late visit?" she asked, genuinely curious.

Her open expression confirmed his suspicions. Even though Sutworth Manor was as close to the border as Highgate End, its lack of leadership left it isolated. She did not yet know.

"It is," he said, glancing at Lawrence, who stepped forward.

"If I may be so bold," his friend said. "A room for the remainder evening would be—"

"Of course!" Clarissa waved a servant forward. "I apologize for not having offered one to you."

He and Lawrence had discussed the possibility of offering to escort her to Dunburg Abbey that very evening, but they'd agreed it may be better to leave at dawn. If the lady agreed. But knowing Clarissa's mind, Aidan expected an argument. She'd likely wish to leave right away, but Aidan did not wish to risk her safety. There'd been word of reivers roaming the area, and they preferred to travel at night.

"Many thanks." Lawrence, ever the gentleman, bowed as he was led away.

"Is there somewhere private—"

Her eyes widened in surprise, but instead of refusing him, she said, "Follow me." Dismissing the lingering servant who had been prepared to show Aidan a room, Clarissa led him away from the entrance.

It was highly inappropriate and more than a bit unusual. But when he gave Clarissa the news, she would care less for propriety than for safety. Even if the servants talked about his visit—and they would—it would not matter.

Clarissa would no longer be their lady tomorrow.

As he followed her up a set of dark, winding stairs, their only guide a wall torch Clarissa had taken up near the first step, the ominous sound of their own footfalls echoed around them. Watching her voluminous gown drag over each step, he wondered why she was fully dressed at such an hour. And what she would say when he told her. And how he could bear to give her up.

They reached a long corridor, and Clarissa pushed open the

first door on their left. Entering the large room behind her, his gaze fell to an interior door that was still ajar . . . the master chamber.

Clarissa's bedchamber.

Hardening at the thought of her lying in bed, her blue gown discarded in favor of a thin shift, or better—

He stopped himself, though watching Clarissa bend down to adjust the wood in the fire in the brazier did nothing to temper his thoughts. Finding a cushioned chair in the otherwise sparsely decorated room, Aidan sat and waited for her to do the same.

Sufficiently separated from her, though not from his desire to touch her, Aidan leaned forward to explain his unconventional visit.

"I've news, my lady."

"Clarissa."

Aidan smiled despite the seriousness of the situation.

"I've news, *Clarissa.*"

He had not meant it to sound quite so . . . intimate. It was the reason he'd avoided using her given name. Every time he did, it reminded him of their first, well, second meeting. Of their time together. Of how often he'd thought of this woman throughout the years.

He watched as she folded her hands in her lap, the creamy skin of her hands so much warmer than the cool blue of the gown beneath them. He knew from experience . . .

Stop!

"The annulment," he said, knowing he needed to tell her but not wanting to alarm her, not wanting to ruin what would be one of their last moments together. "It is done."

As expected, she startled at first. Blinking, Clarissa watched him as if waiting to see if he would take back the words. And then the questions came.

"Done? What do you mean? How do you come by that knowledge?"

He explained everything his sister-in-law had told him, watching as her expression turned from confusion to fear. Bounding up from her seat, Clarissa made for the door before he could stop her.

"I must tell Father—"

"Wait," he said, catching her. He'd meant only to stop her from leaving, not to grab her around the arm. But now that his hand was there, Aidan refused to pull it away. Though he could feel nothing but fabric beneath his fingers, being this close to her inflamed his senses. He could smell the soft lavender scent he knew she preferred.

His intention was merely to relax her, to comfort her, and yet she was no longer married to Lord Stanley. And one persistent thought kept repeating in Aidan's head, no matter how hard he tried to silence it—

Clarissa is mine.

Without thinking, he pulled her to him, reaching up to cup her cheeks in his hands. He paused just long enough for her surprise to fade away and turn into something more.

She swallowed, her eyes wide. Clarissa knew what he was about to do, and she wasn't going to stop him. He tried to be soft, gentle. But when their lips touched, he knew this was so much more than a simple distraction.

He wanted Clarissa to be his in truth.

She mimicked him, her hands on his cheeks, the warm touch overpowered by the sweet softness of her lips. But unlike the first time, he was not content to stop just yet. He touched his tongue to hers, sweeping it from one side to the other until she understood. Clarissa opened ever so slightly for him. She would have stopped there, but Aidan persisted, nudging her to open wider, and when she did, he swallowed her gasp as his tongue finally found hers.

My God. This woman had never been properly kissed. Despite her short marriage to Stanley, she was a virgin in every real way, an innocent so pure that he nearly despised himself for showing her now, on the precipice of her new life, the pleasures that could await.

Even still, he did not stop.

CLARISSA WAS GOING TO FAINT.

She'd never actually fainted, but surely this knee-weakening sensation could only lead to one thing. Engulfed by this man, his hands and mouth so gentle despite his size, Clarissa shuddered with pleasure. She marveled at the sensations, finally understanding what he had meant when he'd called their first kiss chaste.

That could barely have been called a kiss compared to what they were doing now. His mouth slanted over hers, devouring her and rendering her utterly unable, or unwilling, to pull away. When Aidan groaned against her mouth, she moved her hands from his face to his neck, pulling him toward her. Closer. Closer.

Then, completely uninvited, Lord Stanley's words came back to her.

You are unworthy.

He had said the words each time, and though Clarissa had never truly believed them, they had lingered close to the surface of her mind. She pulled away, reminded of her past—and of her future. Aidan would not be hers.

"I—"

"Oh God, Clarissa, I am so sorry."

He thought she was appalled by what had just happened. Clarissa was nothing of the sort, but she dared not repeat her husband's words. Nay, her *former* husband's words.

"Do not apologize," she said, taking a step back and looking down at her feet, unable to meet his gaze. "I . . . enjoyed it."

Very much, she added silently.

"That may be so"—she looked up as he spoke—"but it was not

97

the most honorable way to distract you from the current situation."

"As to that—"

"We cannot travel this eve. It is much too dangerous."

"We?"

She wanted nothing more than to fall back into Aidan's arms. That would certainly do more harm than good, but she really couldn't remember ever wanting anything quite so much . . .

"Lawrence and I will escort you to Dunburg Abbey."

"Nay," she said, shaking her head. "I cannot let you do that. If my father finds out—"

"He will not. We will leave before dawn."

"If he learns of your visit and then finds me at Dunburg—"

"The few who saw us here tonight will be paid handsomely for their silence."

"You will bribe my men to keep quiet?"

"Aye," he said, without apology. "I trust no one else with your safety."

Aidan neither smiled nor backed away from his assertion that only he could be trusted to see her safely installed at Dunburg. For all she knew, it might be true. She hardly knew the men of Sutworth, and if what Aidan had said was true, her father could be on his way here now.

She could not risk staying any longer. But neither did she want to risk Aidan's safety.

"You cannot . . . your clan—"

Aidan's frown deepened. "I told you of Allie?"

"Aye, the one who relayed the message to you."

"She knows I'm here."

"She does?"

Aidan looked as if he wanted to say something more, but he kept silent. A moment later, he said, "None in my clan would see a woman unprotected. I *will* escort you to Dunburg Abbey."

"But I am sure there is someone—"

"I am going."

Stubborn Scot.

"I need to speak to Father Patrick. Tonight." She moved past Aidan once again. This time, he allowed her to pass. When he did not argue with her, she thought perhaps he had stayed behind. But halfway down the corridor, a very real presence behind her made her turn around.

He stood there, stalwart and fierce, and an overwhelming surge of warmth washed over Clarissa. She had never felt so protected. He would not let anyone hurt her, she realized. Except . . . if she managed to reach Dunburg and was accepted by the nuns there, the loss of Aidan de Sowlis, again, would be the very thing that hurt her most.

CHAPTER 12

"The abbess is dead."

Clarissa looked from Father Patrick, who made that announcement, to her two other companions, unsure of what to say. They stood on the outskirts of the abbey.

"Dead?" Lawrence was the first to ask.

They'd sent Father Patrick ahead, a precaution the priest had insisted was unnecessary. Aidan had insisted on it anyway. Until he was sure the nuns at Dunburg were willing to take her in, Clarissa would not show her face to them.

She'd caught Aidan glancing at her as they waited—more than once. Each time, she had looked away, more from sadness than embarrassment. They'd not discussed the kiss. In fact, the last time they'd been alone together had been on the way to Father Patrick's chamber.

"Aye. God rest her soul, she passed a sennight ago, and none have any knowledge of the missive I sent."

He looked directly at her, and before he finished, Clarissa knew it was bad.

"It seems the abbey will be closing. Its benefactor, the Earl of Argyll, founded Dunburg after promising the Creator to do so when he survived a violent storm at sea. With the recent trouble along the borders, the nuns have been unable to sustain the abbey on its own. Their herd of sheep continues to dwindle courtesy of reivers. Without the earl's gold, it cannot survive." Father frowned. "The abbess had convinced the earl to keep the abbey open, but without her, all agree their cause is lost. They are making preparations to leave even now."

It was Father's expression that jolted Clarissa from her frozen state. He looked as if he would weep for her. She glanced at Aidan, and then Lawrence, and tightened her grip on the reins of her mount.

Nay. This could not be.

"There must be others," she said, "mayhap not in Northumbria where my father's influence is too great, but here in Scotland. There must be others who would be willing to—"

"She cannot return to Sutworth Manor," Father Patrick said to Aidan.

Clarissa wanted to scream as the priest ignored her, but she reminded herself Father had been nothing but kind since she'd laid her troubles at his feet. She lived in a world ruled by men, and it would do well for her to remember it.

"Nay," she said, attempting to keep her voice calm, "I will not return to Sutworth, but neither will I go back to England."

Aidan watched her, his shoulders square and chin lifted.

"You will return to Highgate End with me."

"No," she said, as forcefully as she could. "I will not. I've put you, and your cause, in too much danger already. Anyone who saw you at Sutworth—"

Aidan and Father Patrick spoke at the same time.

"I've ensured they will not . . ."

"None will breathe a word of it."

Both men stopped to allow the other to speak. Which was when Lawrence entered the argument. "I will escort the priest back to Sutworth, then return to Highgate End to notify your brother of your whereabouts."

"Aye," Aidan said, turning to his friend. "I will circumvent Sutworth on my return, which will take nearly an extra full day. Tell him I should be back at Highgate End by nightfall tomorrow."

"Wait!" she yelled, feeling her cheeks flush with frustration. "No one is listening to me. I am telling you, I will not go with you, Aidan. I cannot—"

"Aye, there are other places," he said. "But we cannot traipse through the countryside looking for an abbey or convent willing to take you. Our own priest will write—"

"And what of my father?" she demanded.

Aidan and Lawrence exchanged a glance. They were worried, rightly so, but did not want her to know it. Did they think she was dense?

"He will not know you are there. We will keep your visit quiet—"

"Visit?" Clarissa did not mean to yell, but she had long ago begun to panic. If forced to choose between being discovered by her father and being the instrument by which the shaky peace along the border fell apart, though she was still not convinced her father would capitulate, Clarissa would gladly sacrifice herself. "Aidan," she started again more calmly. "Think on this. I cannot go to Highgate End with you."

While she spoke, Father Patrick walked toward Lawrence, who held the reins to his mount. As he prepared himself to leave, Clarissa knew what would happen next. And she was powerless to stop it.

Unless . . . unless she returned with the priest. Gave herself over to her father . . .

"Do not even consider it."

Aidan's knowing glare surprised her.

"You are always welcome at Sutworth Manor," Father Patrick

said. "We are honored to have you as our lady. But if you come with me now, your father *will* find you there."

Oh God, he was really leaving.

"Farewell, lass."

And before she could even consider whether to nudge her mount forward and attempt to accompany them anyway, he and Lawrence were gone. It still had not rained, and the cloud of dust they left behind rose from the ground as if aiding in their disappearance.

Father Patrick was gone.

And she was left with . . .

No, no, no.

This could not possibly be happening.

GRAEME IS GOING to kill me.

And his brother would be justified. He knew better than to bring Clarissa back to Highgate. Lord knew he did. But Aidan could not bear the thought of her returning to her father.

He did not yet know exactly what Lord Stanley had done to her, but it had clearly affected her, as was to be expected. No woman should be forced to endure such treatment, and certainly not one as good and giving as Clarissa.

Glancing to the side of the path, he announced, "We stop here for the night."

As Lawrence had suggested, they'd made a wide berth around Sutworth and would enter Highgate from the east. Aidan hated the idea of sleeping on the road, the exposed section of marshland offering little cover, but they had no choice. He was well known in these parts, and keeping Clarissa's identity a secret was imperative, so they could not seek shelter. Perhaps it would be safest to ride through the night, but Clarissa was exhausted. They'd not slept the evening before, having left Sutworth before dawn.

Their greatest threat sleeping in the wild was from reivers, but luckily this particular stretch of the path was typically not appealing to them. It was too wet for raising sheep, and only patches of dry land like the one they now rode upon made travel even possible.

"Here?"

Clarissa looked around them, sunlight having long since abandoned them, the moonlight as their guide. The only cover, to their left, was a line of trees that marked the entranceway to the Carnwood Mountains. In the daylight, the view was a spectacular combination of rugged Scotland and the open farmlands that marked the central lowlands.

"Aye, lass. We cannot chance you being seen."

They'd not spoken much since leaving Dunburg Abbey. In truth, he had not known what to say, an affliction those close to him would struggle to believe. Taking care of others had always come easily to him, and it gave him great joy. But he hardly knew how to help Clarissa. Stealing her away and hiding her at Highgate End while they found another abbey hardly seemed the best course. But what choice did he have? The alternative was to do the very thing he'd wanted all along—wed her. But to do so would ensure Theffield refused to assist the cause. Indeed, it would all but ensure he'd attack them.

They dismounted, and Aidan pointed to a thicket he could still see from his position. "You can have a bit of privacy over there."

He began to set up camp, and by the time Clarissa returned, he'd fed the horses and had begun to prepare a fire.

"Is that wise?" she asked, pointing at the small pile of wood and kindling.

He nodded behind them. "The river where we watered the horses back there splits into an old Roman road and this less-used path. If it had rained at all in the past sennight, this path would be deluged with water. But even though passable right now, it is hardly traveled."

She watched him without speaking as he finished preparing their camp. With nothing more than stale oatcakes and nuts to offer her, he'd considered hunting for meat but decided the risk of leaving Clarissa was not worth the potential reward. Instead, he unrolled the sole bedroll for his companion, stoked the fire, and patted the rock beside him.

Clarissa lifted her skirts and sat beside him.

"I've a shift in my belongings, but . . ."

"But?" he prompted.

He knew what she was thinking. Aidan could see it in the way she glanced down at her feet. If it were lighter, he would likely see the telltale spots of pink on her cheeks. Now that they had a moment to stop with nothing but quiet around them for miles in every direction, he had been thinking much the same thing.

It was going to be a very long night indeed. He could not have endured watching her sit next to him in such a garment, so he thanked the saints she'd decided against wearing it.

"You've nothing to be embarrassed about, lass. That kiss—"

Her eyes flew up and locked with his own. "How did you know?"

Aidan chuckled, handing her an oatcake that he'd taken from the leather bag at his feet. "That you were thinking of it?"

Clarissa nodded.

"I supposed I didn't. But I've thought of little else myself." He shrugged. "Maybe I hoped the same was true of you."

When her mouth opened and her lips closed down on the oatcake, Aidan wished to trade places with it. He doubted an attacking band of English reivers could have taken his eyes away from her. "I was wrong to have—"

"I liked it," she blurted. "Very much."

Aidan didn't dare move. He'd already promised himself not to let it happen again. There was simply too much at stake. And yet . . .

"As did I, lass."

"I had no idea—"

"Clarissa . . ." How could he put this delicately? "If we continue to discuss the matter, I cannot guarantee it won't happen again."

His heart skipped a beat when she opened her mouth to answer. If she gave him permission . . .

But she must have thought better of it because she took another bite of the oatcake instead, following it with a swig of fresh water from the river they'd passed. When a droplet spilled onto her chin, Aidan wiped it off with his thumb. At least, he did so in his mind. In truth, he'd not moved a muscle.

"It has been like this, with us, from the start."

He knew she didn't say it to provoke him. Or to test his earlier warning. She said it because it was the truth. One he would not deny. Those days at the tournament had been enough for him to know her.

"Aye, lass. It has."

"Is it normal then? When a man and woman—"

"Nay, Clarissa. I have been in the company of many beautiful . . ." That had not come out as intended. Clarissa's raised eyebrows confirmed his blunder. "It is not," he finished simply. And when she smiled, the lines of worry that usually marked the corners of her eyes magically turned to lines of mirth.

It pleased him to see her smile. She should have been allowed more of them in her short life.

He wished to give them to her.

But he could not have what he most wanted. If things had been different, if Lady Clarissa were not the daughter of a man he, his clan, and his country needed on their side . . . but nothing was more important than ensuring the enduring safety of his people.

Still, while she was with him, Aidan would do what he could to ensure that beautiful smile became more frequent than her frowns. He would be the one to restore her faith in men and make her forget at least some of the horrors she'd faced.

And he would begin right now.

CHAPTER 13

"Tell me something I don't know of you already," Aidan said, catching her off guard.

Finished with her modest meal, Clarissa pulled her riding gown beneath her, wishing she were wearing something a bit more comfortable.

"When I was young, I dreamed of being a scullery maid."

The look on his face told her she'd surprised him.

"Surely not—"

"The kitchens have always fascinated me. Unlike my own bedchamber, where I spent much of my time as a child, there was always activity there. People coming and going, the smell of freshly baked bread . . . 'twas my favorite place in the castle. I knew enough to understand it was hard work, but still I dreamed of it. Of having the freedom to come and go each day—"

"Were you not able to spend any time there?"

Another memory assaulted her, one she did not so readily share. One of her father finding her, yet again, in a place that "did not suit to the daughter of an earl."

"Nay," she said simply. "My father forbade it. But no matter, it was an overly romantic notion. The life of any maid is not so easy.

I understand more now than I did as a child—the freedom I so coveted is not easily won." Trying to keep the tone of their conversation light, she nodded to him. "Tell me something of you."

Aidan cocked his head to the side, thinking. "When I was a child, I always wished for a sister."

"You did?"

"Aye. When our mother died, I mourned twofold—for her and for the loss of a dream I'd always thought quite silly."

"Not so silly," she said, "I wished for the same." She smiled. "Or a brother."

"Your father never married again."

"Nay. When I was young and bold, I asked him about it once." She stopped, remembering that particular conversation.

"And what did he say?"

Why did every topic seem to lead back to the man who'd raised her, who hated her?

Clarissa shook her head. She thought Aidan would let the comment pass, but he did not.

"Clarissa? What did he say?"

Her throat tightened. She had never said the words aloud and did not wish to do so now. But that she'd shared some of this with him—knowing Aidan would not condemn her—compelled her to do so anyway. "That I had killed my mother, and I'd not be given another chance to do so again."

She looked down at her hands, folding her fingers inside each other. Taking a deep breath, she was surprised to see Aidan's feet appear in front of her. She hadn't even heard him move. When he squatted in front of her, Clarissa was forced to look up.

Without saying a word, Aidan reached out and covered her hands with his own. A familiar welling inside her chest threatened to give way to the tears she'd shed so many times over her father's treatment of her. But she was determined not to cry this time. There was no reason to do so.

She was not to blame for her mother's death. How many times had Albert and Eda told her that?

She looked up.

Aidan's expression of warmth and understanding nearly shattered her resolve not to break down in tears over her father's cruel words. Again.

"You do not believe that, do you?" he asked softly.

His warm hands reminded her that spring nights in Scotland were much the same as they were in northern England, cool and unforgiving. In that moment, she was glad for it.

"Nay, I do not."

Thought she meant it, Aidan did not appear to believe her. He waited, as if trying to decipher if she would change her mind. Though she said nothing more, he did not move. An awareness that had nothing to do with her father or his words covered her like a thick blanket.

"You've not had it so easy, lass."

She supposed not, but some had fared much worse than she.

"I just want to feel safe." When the words poured out of her, Clarissa realized the truth of them. She'd been running, it seemed, for so long. And now she was doing so again, and she just wanted it to end.

Aidan stood, pulling her with him. His arms encircled her as her own arms reached around him of their own accord. They stood that way for so long, the crackling of the fire the only sound except for their own breathing. Clarissa was loath to break away.

So she didn't.

"You are safe with me," he said finally. "I pledge on my honor as the second to the chief of Clan Scott, I will not let any harm come to you."

He never pulled away, and Clarissa did not see his face when he said the words, but she did not need to. She knew he meant every word. This time, she could not stop the tears from springing to her eyes.

"Do you understand what I'm saying, lass?"

She nodded against his chest.

"You are under my protection. My clan's protection."

"But—"

He did look at her then, his gaze so intense that Clarissa would have been frightened if he were foe rather than friend.

"You will come to Highgate End and stay there until your safety can be assured."

"None can know I am there."

"Very few will know, aye."

"And you will help me find a convent that will take me?" She'd already asked so much of him, but Clarissa was truly at his mercy. And though she'd sworn never to be at the mercy of another man, she trusted Aidan.

"I will." He frowned. Aidan did not like her plan, but he would not go back on his promise. For the first time that she could remember, she actually believed all might be well.

Reluctant to leave the warmth of his embrace, Clarissa laid her head against his chest once more, thanking God for sending him to her. Her husband had been just as wrong as her father. If God wished to punish her for being unworthy, surely Aidan wouldn't have returned to her life just when she needed him most.

THE SCENT of her lingered still.

Aidan looked up at Highgate Castle, so named given for the mound of earth that perched the circular structure high above the surrounding land. Breathing deeply, he closed his eyes for a brief moment, allowing himself to remember last eve, and how it had felt to hold the woman who now rode beside him. He'd wanted her, aye, but for far more than that he'd wanted them to stay that way—nestled together, her clutching the fabric at his back as he struggled to get closer to her. She fit perfectly against him, as if she belonged there. He'd only released her upon remembering how badly she needed to sleep.

Sleep.

Once Clarissa was installed safely at Highgate, he desperately needed rest. He'd stayed awake for the second night, not trusting the silence of the road he'd thought was safe. It had been, but Aidan did not take his oath to Clarissa lightly. In order to properly protect her, he could not sleep until they were safely inside Highgate's walls. With all that had happened recently along the border, he could not be too careful.

"Do you remember what I told you?" he asked, glancing over at her.

Peeking out from under the hooded cape she'd worn as a blanket last eve, Clarissa nodded. Looking down and ensuring her face could not be seen, she followed him up the incline and through the gates of his home. If any of the guards thought it odd his companion wore such a garment in the middle of the day, none of them commented. In fact, no one questioned them at all as he rode past the stables, where he'd normally stop, and led her directly to the Prison Tower. Each of the four towers framing Highgate Castle had once had a purpose, though this one served as a prison no longer. Before he was born, it had been converted into a mostly abandoned series of chambers for guests, used only when the great keep and the other three towers were filled to capacity.

The furthest away from the keep, situated at Highgate's southeast corner, the Prison Tower also had its own well to recommend it. But Aidan had mostly chosen it for Clarissa because of the smells that made their way to it from the nearby bakehouse. If Clarissa had enjoyed being in the kitchen back at Theffield, certainly she would like to meet Lewis, Highgate's baker and one of the few people Aidan would trust with her true identity.

When they were directly in front of the entrance to the tower, Aidan dismounted and helped Clarissa do the same. Aidan pushed open the iron-studded door, revealing a set of winding stairs on the east wall of the rounded tower.

"The garderobe is on the ground floor," he said, pointing to an interior door as they passed it. "And this," he led the way to the first landing, "is one of four bedchambers within this tower. I would suggest the next one up"—he continued upward—"so that you have this."

Waiting for Clarissa to catch up to him, Aidan ducked under an archway that led directly to a wall-walk. Though no guards were in sight, he planned to station a friendly and unobtrusive one in the vicinity. He pointed beneath them.

"From here there is no danger of being noticed from below. Most of the activity in the inner courtyard will be behind us."

"The view . . . 'tis so beautiful."

The rolling green hills had always been his favorite scenery from this vantage point, but even after two days of travel, the road-weary woman who stood beside him stole that honor.

"Don't you agree?" she asked, her voice full of wonder.

He could not tear his gaze from her. "Aye, lass. I do."

The glimmer in her eyes told him she had realized that he spoke not of the landscape but of her. Clarissa opened her mouth to respond when an unwelcome voice from behind them interrupted them.

"You found your way home, brother."

Clarissa whipped her head around as Aidan waited for Graeme to continue.

"My lady," Graeme addressed her. "Well met since those many years past when I greeted you in your hall at Theffield."

In deference to his position as chief, Clarissa curtsied prettily, as if they'd just met at court.

"Chief," she said, "the honor is mine."

Graeme nodded politely but did not waste a moment. He gestured toward the inner chamber of the tower, and Clarissa followed him inside. Aidan did the same. Once they were all sequestered inside the very room Aidan had suggested Clarissa take for her own, he closed the door behind them.

"We received word from your father just this morn," Graeme began, addressing Clarissa.

She seemed surprised. And frightened. Graeme must have belatedly realized the implication of his words. "His message was not about you, my lady. I'm sorry for the misunderstanding."

Graeme glanced at Aidan and then addressed his next words directly to Clarissa. "He has agreed to assist our cause."

No news could have been more surprising. He had been convinced the earl would do otherwise. And while this should have been a cause for celebration, it was not.

Clarissa's face drained of color. "If he finds out that I am here—"

"He will not," Aidan cut in. "This is welcome news," he said to Graeme. "But it changes nothing. As I'm sure Lawrence told you, Lady Clarissa has nowhere to go. With Dunburg Abbey shutting its doors, we must help her find somewhere else to go."

And just so that his brother understood the situation clearly, he added, "Until then, she is under our protection. I will speak with Lewis, who can assist our cause. Malcolm will need to station guards we can trust with this secret—"

"There is not one man or woman here I would not trust with my life," Graeme interrupted.

"I agree," Aidan said, "but it is not our lives we are discussing. It is Lady Clarissa, our entire clan, and indeed, all of the borderers for whom her identity must remain a secret."

He watched his brother contemplate his words. Graeme had not flinched when he'd announced Clarissa was under their protection. His brother would honor the vow he'd made, of course, but Aidan had expected more of a reaction.

"Very well," Graeme said. "I leave her protection to you. In the meantime, we've much to discuss."

"Aye, we do. I will be along shortly."

Graeme turned to leave but stopped at the door. "I will send Gillian along," he said with a final nod to Clarissa. "She looks forward to meeting you."

Aidan turned to explain that he would be back after his meeting with Graeme and that Lady Gillian would attend to her needs in the meantime. But Clarissa's pallor and wide eyes stopped him. She appeared as shocked as if she'd seen a fairie.

"What is it, lass?"

Clarissa opened her mouth but nothing came out.

Aidan's heartbeat quickened. "What is it—"

"He . . . he did not question you. Or order you to send me away. He . . . your brother . . ."

His shoulders sagged with relief. For a moment he'd thought something was wrong.

"I told you," he clarified. "You are under my protection, which means you are under the clan's protection as well. My word and my brother's are interchangeable," he explained.

Aidan wanted to stay to assure her that she was safe, and that her father's decision did not change that. But Graeme was right, there was much to be done. "Rest," he said. "Lady Gillian will be along shortly. And I will visit you as soon as I'm able."

Then, because he could not stop himself, Aidan leaned over and placed the gentlest of kisses on her lips. If the move startled her, Clarissa did not show it. But as he turned to leave, Aidan could have kicked himself. Why had he done that? Though it nearly killed him, he had not kissed her at all during their journey . . . since the kiss they'd shared at Sutworth had nearly undone him, of course. And yet, it had seemed the most natural thing in the world to say farewell in that way.

Clarissa is not yours to kiss anytime you please, and you will do well to remember that.

God help him, he was trying. Though it was becoming harder and harder each passing day.

CHAPTER 14

"She is absolutely lovely."

Gillian waved her hand in front of him, but Aidan was too engrossed in his thoughts to form a response. They sat in the hall, the evening meal being cleaned around them. Graeme had already left the head table to address the steward's concern over an accounting error that could have waited for tomorrow. As always, the hall was just a bit quieter without Allie's presence, though she and Reid would no doubt be back before long.

But Graeme never liked leaving problems unsolved. He had difficulty sleeping unless all was well, at least for the moment. Their mother had been the same way, and whenever their father had left on a counter-raid or for battle, he and his brother had refused to leave her side, knowing she'd never sleep if left alone. The memory of being curled up by her side as a laddie would never leave him, no matter how much time passed.

The illness had taken her five years ago, but the loss felt so fresh some days, as if he'd only just learned of her death.

"Aidan?"

He shifted his focus to his sister-in-law.

"Aye?" And then he stood, suddenly worried. "Are you ill? Do you—"

"Nay, nay. Sit," she said. "I seem to go longer and longer without the need to have a chamber pot by my side. I was speaking of Lady Clarissa."

Clarissa. More than a day had passed since he'd arrived at Highgate End with his new ward. He'd returned to the Prison Tower after his meeting with Graeme, who'd informed him about the next steps of Douglas's plan, only to find Gillian with Clarissa. Much to his chagrin, his sister-in-law had waved him away, assuring him she was well taken care of for the night.

This morning, unable to stay away, he'd introduced Clarissa to Lewis, the baker, and the secret path beneath the Prison Tower that led to the bakehouse. He wasn't sure if she or Lewis were more delighted at the arrangement. She could work alongside him, if she liked, and Clarissa had wasted no time expressing her excitement. He'd given her a key and advised her to lock the door behind her. Though the doors of the tower normally remained open, he wanted to keep Clarissa's presence as secret as possible.

"She is lovely," Gillian said, repeating herself.

"I'm sorry, Gill."

He took a swig of ale and wondered if it was too soon to visit her. Gillian's maid knew a mystery woman was in residence, as did Fiona, an older servant who doted on his sister-in-law and had been serving Highgate for as many years as he'd been alive. Between all three women, it would be a wonder if Clarissa had any privacy or rest if they did discover her identity.

"I hope you will not be upset with her," Gillian sat back in her chair, "but Allie told me of your discussion about the annulment before she left."

He took another swig. "As I suspected she would." In fact, it was easier that way. He had no desire to tell the tale again. "But much has happened since I left for Sutworth."

Gillian raised her brows. "Clearly."

She stopped talking when a servant walked by them.

"How long do you think it will be before Father Simon sends word?"

They'd agreed to elicit the support of Clan Kerr's priest, their own too new to Highgate for Aidan's liking. Though Gillian thought it absurd that he did not fully trust their priest, he was not taking any chances. He'd sent Malcolm, a trusted warrior who did not ask questions, to Brockburg to seek out Allie and explain the latest developments in Clarissa's situation. Aidan had no doubt Father Simon would help them, and that he would do so as efficiently, or more so, as Sutworth's priest.

In fact, that was exactly what bothered him. Malcolm would return any moment, beginning another countdown to Clarissa's new life as a child of God. As absurd a notion as anything he'd ever heard. Aidan had told his brother as much, but Graeme had reminded him she could not stay here. Any who harbored Theffield's daughter would pay for their interference tenfold.

"Knowing him as I do," he said, sighing, "I do not expect it to be long."

Gillian leaned in toward him. "I spoke with Graeme last eve," she whispered. "And I know you feel, and she feels, there is no other way. But I've been thinking—"

Aidan groaned, knowing where this conversation was heading. "A dangerous prospect."

She swatted his arm. "Be serious. I've been thinking . . . of course if Theffield caught a Scotsman hiding his daughter, he would be quite angry."

Aidan laughed. He was unable to help himself. "Quite angry? Gillian, you don't know the man. He would be infuriated enough to start the war that Caxton has been seeking."

Gillian did not seem concerned by the possibility. In fact, her attitude reminded him quite a bit of Allie's.

"Aye, well. As I said, he would be quite angry—"

Aidan rolled his eyes.

"But what of asking the Waryns for help in hiding her?"

This was one of the things he loved most about Gillian. She was both smart and resourceful, not unlike the woman he loved, who had thus far successfully avoided succumbing to one of the most powerful men in Northumbria.

"I've thought of that," he said, "and the Earl of Clave as well."

Both families, though English, were considered allies. With Geoffrey Waryn's marriage to the Earl of Kenshire's daughter, the Waryns were as powerful as Clarissa's father.

"Eventually, he will find her. A woman such as Clarissa cannot remain in hiding forever. She is not easily forgotten or over-looked. Only the church would have the authority to keep her against his will."

"But it could give her time—"

"And what do you suppose her father will do when he discovers our allies have been harboring his daughter?" Aidan tried to remember to keep his voice low. Though only a handful of men and servants remained in the hall, he did not want to be overheard. "It would not matter that her supporters were English. Theffield knows which side the Waryns fight for. And Clave too. We are united in our efforts to uphold the treaty against men who care more for their personal gain, like Caxton . . . or Theffield, than they do their countries. Scottish. English. It hardly matters any longer."

Gillian looked exactly as he felt.

Defeated.

"Graeme says there is to be a meeting between Douglas and Theffield. A miracle they've both agreed to it after their difficulties in the past."

"Aye," he said, wondering when it would be safe to see Clarissa. He could easily get to the Prison Tower through the—

"And you truly believe Theffield will force Caxton to step down?"

Nay, he should wait until dark. They could not be too careful, and there was already enough coming and going from the tower.

"You are not listening," she accused, arching her eyebrows.

Guilty.

"Go to her already. None will notice. And perhaps I can find someone to speak with who will actually listen to me." Gillian tucked a lock of hair behind her ear.

Hell, he'd waited long enough.

"I'm going to see her."

Now, what in God's name was so funny about that?

CLARISSA TRIED to wash using the scented water Morgan had left behind. Though she was grateful for Lady Gillian's maid, she could not help but wish for a proper bath. She'd been too long without one, but such a luxury simply was not possible. Too many servants would be required to assist in the preparations. It would draw undue attention to her, and Clarissa did not want to endanger the de Sowlis family and Clan Scott.

Morgan had helped her remove her gown, but the long-sleeved cotton shift would have to be discarded next. She was preparing to do just that, when a knock at the door stopped her. The circular room was not so large that even a soft knock wouldn't reverberate through the stone-walled chamber. Pushing her arms back through the sleeves, she opened the door, expecting to find Morgan again.

It was certainly not the maid.

Aidan, dressed casually in dark brown trewes and a cream tunic with its sleeves rolled to his elbows, filled the doorway. She was so distracted by the muscles in his forearms that it took a moment for her to remember her own state of undress.

Backing into the chamber, she tried to appear unaffected as she grabbed the first garment that she spotted, the hooded cloak she'd worn as they rode into Highgate End, and tossed it over her shoulders.

"May I come in?"

She turned toward the sound of his voice, which had become increasingly familiar and comforting.

"Of course," she said, feeling absurd as she pulled the cloak tighter around her chest.

Something had shifted between them the night he'd held her by the fire. A new intimacy had sprung up between them that had left her both sad and confused. She knew Aidan had solicited the help of Clan Kerr's priest; Gillian had told her. She tried to think it a good thing, for the longer she was here, the longer she put his cause in danger, and yet . . .

He looked at the bowl perched on the sole table in the room.

"Your needs have been met, I trust?"

"Aye, of course."

Of course. Could she utter another phrase besides that one? When he was near, Clarissa had difficulty turning her thoughts into coherent words.

"Can I get you anything else?"

She followed his gaze to the bowl and sighed. "Nay, you've been more than gracious—"

"A bath, perhaps?"

He was jesting!

"Surely you cannot . . . that is, it would cause too much fuss—"

That smile. She was sure no one could resist it.

"A tub would be difficult . . ."

"I assumed as much."

"But that is not the only way to cleanse oneself."

The washbowl? But she'd already used it.

"There is a river just down the hill, behind an area the men use to train."

"A river?"

Clarissa had never bathed in a river. She'd crossed one only once, on her way to the tournament, but she'd been on horseback then. She remembered the sunlight's reflection on the shallow water, and how the flow of it entranced her. She'd laughed when her horse kicked up spray onto her gown.

"I will warn you, lass. It's more than a wee bit cold this time of year. But it can be—"

"Aye!" She did not need to hear more. "I will do it."

Would she ever get the chance to bathe in a river again? Likely not. Clarissa smiled at the idea of nuns undressing on a riverbank, preparing to—

"I wish you would smile more often." He said it softly, almost like a prayer.

Clarissa lifted her chin. "'Tis easy to do with you."

"Then come." He took her hand. "A bath and another smile. I promise to give you both this eve."

A shiver of excitement ran through her as she imagined an alternate meaning for his words.

CHAPTER 15

*A*dd this decision to the litany of my mistakes since Clarissa
appeared in that courtyard asking for assistance.

As he led her through the corridors that would deposit them
directly in front of the gatehouse, Aidan had plenty of time to
ponder the events of the day, including this hasty invitation to the
river, which would do nothing to put distance between him and
Clarissa.

Gillian's question plagued him. Was there another way? No
matter how much he wished there were, he doubted it. He'd
already considered the possibility she'd suggested, only to throw
it out. Involving the Waryns or Clave would endanger their negotiations with Theffield—and endanger their friends. His logical
mind assured him Clarissa had devised the safest plan possible—
and yet he could not accept it.

"This way," he said, pushing the thoughts aside.

They exited just inside the gate. Aidan looked back to ensure
Clarissa was well hidden behind him, then called to the guard.
When the portcullis was lifted, he hurried her toward the path
he'd shown Allie back when their training sessions with the
longsword were still a secret. Though they'd never met this late in

the evening, with only the moonlight to guide them, he and Allie had taken this footpath most evenings before supper.

Clarissa caught up to him as they bounded down the hill. When she passed him, he had to run to catch up. Evading him, she ran faster. Aidan would have let her best him, but the lass didn't know where she was going. So he ran ahead and guided her past the training yard and toward the river. When they reached its banks, both of them out of breath, the beautiful sound of her laughter filled the air.

"A gentleman would have let the lady win," she said, the hood of her cape having long since fallen.

"And where, precisely, would you have run to, my lady? Or have you been here before without the pleasure of my company?"

"If I've been here, it was only in a dream," she said. Then, perhaps realizing the implication of her words, she added, "No, I've not been here before and would have likely led us astray."

You could never lead me astray.

Aidan dismissed the thought as that of a sentimental fool, and walked toward the river's edge. "As I said, my lady, it will not be a warm, luxurious bath. The water is cold, especially this time of year."

Or any time of year, really. Even in the summer months, Aidan never stayed in the water for long. He hated cold water. Always had.

"Is it safe?"

Though the moon was high and nearly full, the darkness of the surrounding woods and foreboding current, which was nothing to dismiss, lent the night an air of foreboding.

"Aye," he said. "We'd not be here otherwise. But I will go in with you to be sure."

He began to lift the hem of his shirt when Clarissa stopped him.

"Pardon?"

Of course. He should explain. "You should remove your cape and boots. I will do the same—"

"But you're not wearing a cape."

Her eyes looked as wide as the moon. Aidan scolded himself. She may have been married, but Clarissa was still very much innocent.

"I will remove only my shirt," he explained, "and will be with you the entire time."

Aidan moved to take off his leather boots, reminding her to do the same, and then removed his shirt. He waited for Clarissa to disrobe, telling himself he was strong enough to do this.

She is not yours to claim.

But it seemed the reminder was not necessary, or at least not yet. With her feet bare, Clarissa did not move.

She was staring at his chest.

Aidan had been admired before. Many times, in fact. But never had a woman's gaze made him feel quite like this. Clarissa's lips parted, and she did not move to hide the fact that she very much appreciated what she saw. Not surprisingly, Aidan responded. He hardened, watching her. Neither of them moved.

"Surely you've seen men in this state. In training?" He did not wish to speak Lord Stanley's name, and while he was not an arrogant man, he knew there was a difference between the body of a warrior and that of an old layabout.

Clarissa shook her head. "I'd never been allowed near the training yard."

Christ's toes . . . he couldn't help himself.

"If you continue to stare at me, lass—"

She immediately turned her head. "I'm sorry for being so rude."

He took a step toward her.

"I just—" Her sharp intake of breath when he grabbed her wrist and brought her hand toward his chest sent a jolt of lust through him, though Aidan ignored it. He would not touch her. *Good God, man. Then why are you guiding her hand to you?*

"You are not rude, but curious. And you've a right to be so, Clarissa."

When she met his eyes, he nodded, giving her permission to do as she would. When he removed his hand from hers, he held his breath, waiting.

Splaying her fingers out across his chest, she moved them over the muscles that twitched beneath the feather-light touch of her fingertips. He knew where they were headed. Sure enough, she traced them downward, not quite caressing but definitely exploring each ridge of his stomach. He forced himself to take deep, even breaths.

"'Tis nothing like Lord Stanley."

If anything could have tempered his reaction to her touch, it was that. Aidan covered her hand lest she move any lower.

"I would expect not."

He watched her eyes as they darted downward and then back up to his own.

"Talk to me, my love."

Those last words slipped out, and Aidan silently prayed Clarissa would not notice, or comment.

"He tried thrice to beget a child from me."

When she closed her eyes and tried to pull away, Aidan would not let her.

"He bade me remove my clothes." She opened her eyes. "I did, lying still so as to not anger him. Each time he hovered over me, touching himself and cursing me."

Aidan wasn't sure if he hated Theffield or her former husband more.

"His anger lasted for days. After the third time, he sent his physician to examine me."

She attempted to shift her gaze to the ground, but he tipped her chin up. He wouldn't let her look down. There was nothing for her to be ashamed of.

"Though it was confirmed I was as untouched as my father had promised him, Stanley told the priest otherwise. I did not realize it at first." She shrugged. "But now I know he spun that tale to ensure the annulment would be granted."

When she finished, Clarissa seemed stronger, as if she'd exorcised something that had preyed on her. No longer tentative, her hand began to move again, stroking his chest.

"I am glad to be away from there. From him."

"And I am glad you trusted me with your story."

Foolishly, he brought Clarissa's other hand up to his chest.

"Replace those memories with a new one," he heard himself saying. Untying the laces at her neck, Aidan pushed the thick cape away from her, not daring to look down. Instead, he closed the space between them and captured her mouth in a slow, sensual kiss. One that promised to begin to erase the horrors of her past.

One that risked changing everything.

As her lips opened for him, her tongue touching his tentatively, Aidan wanted so much more than to be inside her.

Of course, he wanted that too.

But he also wanted her to know nothing the terrible men in her life had said was true. She was perfect, just as she was. And Aidan wanted her to know there was good in the world, men who did not treat women poorly simply because they had power, or felt powerless themselves.

He wanted her to know he loved her.

Startling himself with the thought, he pulled back and led her toward the bath he'd promised. As she stepped into the river, he laughed at her intake of breath. The water was indeed frigid.

"Careful." He guided her to the flattest part of the riverbed, a spot he knew well, then reached into a pouch sewn into his trewes and pulled out the scented soap he'd scooped up from Clarissa's bedchamber.

"Here." He handed it to her as she waded further in, submerged to her hip. "You'll want to be quick about it."

"Thank you."

He watched as she took the soap from his hands. And then, before he could stop her, Clarissa dunked herself into the water. Though he still held her hand, the darkness swallowed up everything else until she emerged a moment later.

Pulling away from him, she made quick work of using the soap to wash her hair and face. Reaching under the soaking wet shift, she continued to cleanse herself as Aidan attempted not to look at the hardened nipples that called to him from just beneath the thin fabric.

He finally noticed she was struggling to hold the soap and cleanse her hair and belatedly took it from her, indicating she should turn around. Running it through the long tresses he'd ached to touch for days, he used his fingers to separate the strands and nearly dropped to his knees when she released a soft moan.

"That feels so good," she said. "Nothing at all like it does when Eda washes it."

He nearly forgot how cold the water felt. Keeping a tawdry retort to himself, he finished his ministrations and watched as she slipped beneath the surface again, as nubile as a selkie. When she re-emerged, Aidan did the same, washing quickly and pulling her from the increasingly frigid water.

Dressing quickly, he thanked the saints Clarissa was once again covered with her cloak.

"Now what do we do?"

He looked up toward where the castle was located beyond the tree line, knowing he was a cad for what was about to happen next. The lass was quick, and this time she knew the destination. He smiled in anticipation of her reaction.

"Now," he said, ensuring she was ready to leave. "We run."

STILL LAUGHING as she caught up to him just outside the gate-house, Clarissa chastised the man she'd previously thought more chivalric than any English knight.

"You bested me only because you cheated."

Pulling her cloak back over her head, Clarissa followed Aidan to the entrance of her small chamber in the tower that had become her temporary home.

"Och, a harsh sentiment when I simply wanted to ensure you did not catch an early death." Aidan pushed her gently into the room. "Go, warm up by the fire," he said, turning as if to leave.

"What of you? Will you catch your own death on the way back to the keep?"

He winked, a boyish gesture that made him appear younger, especially when coupled with his wet, wavy hair.

"I will be fine," he said, turning away again.

Clarissa did not want him to leave and told him so.

"You can warm yourself in here."

Aidan's grin fled from his face. "Clarissa, do you understand—"

"I understand I do not wish you to leave." Well, she understood more than that, but it was all she was willing to put into words.

Aidan stood as still as a wooden pell, watching her. Waiting, but for what? For her to change her mind?

On this, I will not change course.

He looked back toward the direction they'd come, then at the fire that roared in the brazier Morgan had cleaned and prepared. He was going to leave, which was just as well.

He *should* leave.

But, may all the saints forgive her, she didn't want him to.

He reached her in three strides, the door slamming behind him so powerfully Clarissa was sure it had cracked at the hinges. Whether she shivered from the cold, her wet shift, or his swift and sure movements as he released the cloak from her shoulders, Clarissa did not care.

He looked down for the briefest of moments, and the groan

that escaped his lips ensured their path forward. She could no longer deny that Aidan de Sowlis was, and had always been, the man to whom she would give her favor. The only one.

Though she knew what he would do next, it was still a shock when he reached for the hem of her shift and lifted it over her head in one smooth movement. She wore nothing beneath it.

Clarissa was utterly and completely bare to his gaze.

"Oh God."

His hands were everywhere at once. On her breasts, cupping and pinching as her mounds molded to his hands. She should be embarrassed, but her thoughts were elsewhere—Clarissa wanted to see him the same way, stripped bare. When his lips moved down her neck, she pulled up the shirt he'd already discarded once that evening, and thankfully, he obliged her by removing it.

And then he pressed up against her, his hard chest slamming against her breasts. Gasping, she was about to comment on the sensation when he drowned her response with a kiss so consuming that Clarissa forgot to breath. His tongue tousled with her own, and she moaned against him. In response, Aidan bit her lower lip, hard enough that she was nearly tempted to bite back.

But she couldn't, for his fingers had found her core. Clarissa couldn't think. She couldn't breathe. She couldn't do anything other than will herself to remain standing. Without warning, those clever fingers entered her, his palm pressing against her as his fingers moved in rhythm with his mouth.

Oh dear God. I cannot take much more.

And yet she wanted more. She wanted it all.

"Listen to me," he whispered in her ear, his words a soft caress to the much harder thrusting down below. "When I whisper the words, you will let go. Forget everything and give yourself to me completely."

She didn't know, or care, what he spoke of. Clarissa only wanted him to keep touching her that way. Forever. So she agreed, nodding mutely, unable to speak.

"Mo rúnsearc, you are mine."

With those words, he pressed against her with all of him—his body, his hand, his lips—all pressing against her in unison, overwhelming her senses with pleasure. She could hold on no longer.

"Now," he demanded, and she knew what he'd meant.

Clarissa gave everything to this man who'd torn her life apart. Who'd shattered every wall she'd built. Touched her in a way that no one else ever had, or would, again. She screamed, or tried to, but his mouth covered hers, the sound drowned by the delicious pressure.

And when her body finally relaxed, the spasms abating little by little, only one coherent thought remained.

She could never, ever, become a nun.

CHAPTER 16

"Graeme, before you leave—"

They'd just finished the morning meal, which would typically be Graeme's cue to lock himself away with the steward for the remainder of the morning. Gillian had already left the hall to look for her maid, and Aidan would be expected to spend his day training the men.

But after last night, he knew he could no longer stay the course with Clarissa. They needed a new plan. One that would keep Clan Scott and the other border clans safe and not require him to forsake Clarissa.

"What ails you, brother?"

They walked out of the hall together, Aidan leading the way toward the pentice that traveled the length of the entrance to the great hall and kitchens. The covered walkway connected to Highgate End's chapel. The courtyard bustled with activity, men preparing for training, servants carrying supplies, and children . . . Aidan watched as a boy tried to pick up an errant chicken. Both he and Graeme laughed at the spectacle.

Finally, he answered his brother.

"I love her," he said simply. The implications of those words, and what he aimed to do about them, were so far-reaching, Aidan knew he would be testing the bounds of his brother's friendship and his chief's tolerance.

"I know you do."

They stopped just before the small chapel and watched as the boy tried again, eliciting a chorus of angry clucks.

"She does not deserve such treatment—"

"No one does, Aidan. Not Lady Clarissa nor any other woman or man. Theffield is a bastard of the worst kind. He trifles with lives just as surely as Caxton does. His daughter is only one of many he'd forsake for his own gain."

Though they stood away from the activity, their conversation private, Aidan could not help but glance in every direction before answering.

"I cannot conceive of a solution yet." His hand moved toward the dirk at his side. Aidan always felt better knowing it was there. "Giving her over to a convent is no longer an acceptable one."

The chief, and not the brother, watched him. Most men would cower under such intense scrutiny, but Aidan was accustomed to the stare. It was the same one their father had given them as boys whenever he wanted them to agree with him.

Indeed, his brother had never looked more like their father than he did in this moment. He was so proud of the man he'd become. He would have smiled if Graeme were not so serious.

"I would not willingly put you and Gillian, and the babe, in danger."

"You offered your protection to the very woman who could see negotiations break apart."

"Aye."

"That protection extends from the clan, so she is one of us now."

Aidan's chest swelled with gratitude. "Aye."

Still scrutinizing him in that intense way, Graeme said, "And so we will protect her."

He had not doubted his brother would say as much, but if he had a plan, Aidan would sorely love to hear it.

"How?"

Graeme's exaggerated sigh did not bode well. "Is it possible Theffield already suspects you?"

"I do not believe so. Everything I saw at Sutworth Manor tells me they despise Theffield more than anyone. The priest claims they will not speak, and I believe him. There are no other ties to me."

He deserved that look. The one that said, *You took an unnecessary risk.* For a man who'd always been so careful, particularly when it came to his clan, Aidan knew he'd acted the part of a lovesick fool when he'd ridden to Sutworth that night. Though Theffield had not been on their heels—he was reportedly meeting Douglas in England, which indicated he had never even left his estate—Aidan would likely have made the same decision again.

"Then we wait." Graeme crossed his arms.

"She cannot stay in that tower indefinitely." Aidan already felt poorly about asking her to hide away for a few days longer. She'd spent so much of her life in relative captivity.

"If he learns she is here before he gets rid of Caxton, he will renege."

"And when I marry her?"

They'd both known what Aidan intended, but saying the words aloud sent a rush through him. He felt . . . empowered.

"We must hope the new warden will not be so easily manipulated as Caxton."

"But Theffield will never accept me. Nor our clan. He will take my actions —"

"Our actions."

"He will take our actions as an insult and will likely call for the very war we aim to avoid."

"Well, brother," he said, clapping him on the back. "The only question that remains is whether you are prepared to go to war over the woman you love."

He was prepared to battle the devil himself for Clarissa, but his safety was not the only thing at stake. "Nay, the question is whether I am prepared to put our clan in danger for her."

Graeme leveled that look at him again, giving him a moment to think. Aidan squeezed the handle of his dirk. He thought of Gillian, and Allie. Of his duty to them, and to his brother. He lived to protect them. Did he dare put them in danger? Claiming Clarissa as his own would lead to death and destruction, unless her father could somehow be convinced the match was a good one.

Did he even dare?

"I think," he said, knowing what Clarissa would say, "I have another idea."

"No."

Clarissa sat on the edge of the bed, staring at him in shock. Surely he couldn't think such a thing possible. "You've risked everything for me, and I cannot allow you to continue doing so. Hiding me here . . . that is dangerous enough. But what you're proposing would start a war."

"Nay." He stood and began to pace. "I aim to avoid one. Once your father and Douglas negotiate the terms of—"

"He will not agree."

Aidan sighed, presumably in frustration.

Well, it was nothing less than she'd been feeling all day. After he left the night before, Clarissa had hardly slept. And though she'd had a lovely conversation with Lady Gillian and spent an enjoyable day in the bakehouse with Lewis, her every thought had been focused on the man who now stood in front of her.

"What do you mean 'he will not agree'?"

What could she possibly say? That she loved a man her father would never accept? Which was precisely why Aidan's idea was such a poor one.

"Aidan, I doubt he will even treat with Douglas. He's likely just toying with him. He desires prestige, aye, but my father cares for power above all else. The king—"

"Is ill and will likely die."

Clarissa winced. He was her king, not his, and therefore it was not treasonous for Aidan to comment on his likely fate so bluntly. Even so, she knew he was right. She'd heard the whispers.

"I should say, then, the king's *advisors* would be cross with my father if he were to oust one of the king's favorites, even if he has the authority to do so. I know what he's said but—" She shrugged, less and less sure of her convictions. Perhaps she was wrong. "My father has spent his life garnering favor with the king. 'Tis the only thing he cares about more than expanding the holdings that will one day go to the babe I am not carrying. Which is why he will never, ever allow me to marry a Scot. With no other heirs, Theffield will pass to me. A woman. And he will not allow that either."

Aidan's eyes widened. "What if you relinquished your claim?"

"I would do so, gladly. But don't you understand? If that happens, Theffield will revert back to the crown upon his death, and that will mean my father has lost."

And Father never, ever loses.

"Look at me, Clarissa."

He moved too close for her not to do so. Her heart hammered in her chest, ignoring her attempts to calm it. "I cannot stay."

"But neither can you leave."

"My father—"

"Can be dealt with. Before his meeting with Douglas. After. I care not. Surely you realize that this—" he gestured to both of them, "—happens just once in a lifetime."

She wanted to agree. Clarissa had never wanted anything

more than to throw herself into Aidan's arms and forget that her father could be coming for her even now.

"You are wrong," she said, her voice small but her heart filled with love. "It has happened once before," she rushed to clarify, needing to smooth the furrow in his brow, "at the Tournament of the North when a very handsome Scotsman looked at me as if I were the most beautiful woman in the stands."

"In all of England, and all of Scotland too. And that was before I knew you as I do now."

"And then I let you go."

"Nay." He grabbed her hands. "You did not let me go. Your father forced you to leave."

"As he will do again."

Aidan's shoulders sagged. "We will find a way."

Clarissa wished she shared his conviction. She got to her feet. "And what of Highgate End? And Lady Gillian and Allie? Your niece or neph—"

"What of you, Clarissa? Do you not matter as much as they do?"

In truth, she was not sure that she did.

"Aidan—"

He kissed her before she could finish. This kiss was unlike the others they'd shared. It was less frantic, his lips opening hers like a flower's petals in spring. Soft and slow, until his tongue took over her mouth. It circled her upper lip and then the lower, reverently, and then finally found her own. Like before, a fluttering ran from her chest to her stomach and then lower. When his hands moved up to her head, holding it in place as he continued his gentle assault, Clarissa wrapped her arms around him lest she fall to the ground.

He'd certainly mastered helping her forget their troubles.

"Open wide for me, my love."

Clarissa thought she had already, but when she did as he instructed, his mouth slanted over hers and took even more. So this was what it meant to be consumed by someone. She met each thrust of his tongue as his hands moved swiftly from her head to her bottom. As he pulled her toward him, Clarissa clung to him. She could clearly feel him against her, and she knew unequivocally what he tried to tell her.

Throbbing with need and aware of Aidan in a way she could not explain, Clarissa felt her shoulders heave with an exertion that was hardly warranted. She had done nothing but stand there, and yet she may as well have run up the very hill they'd raced on last eve.

"And this," she said, somehow *knowing*, "this happens but once in a lifetime."

Aidan smiled, a slow sensuous smile that promised so much.

"Twice, I've been told."

She laughed then, so hard she was sure the guards outside could hear her. And she did forget everything, save the sweet sound of Aidan's laughter as the faintest of lines appeared around the corners of his eyes.

A laugh that was abruptly cut off by a sudden and incessant knock at the door.

CHAPTER 17

"*I* would rather sink my dirk into his black heart than cower before him."

Aidan paced in Graeme's solar, back and forth, as he'd been doing since his brother had come to fetch him from Clarissa's chamber.

"I can go in your stead—"

"No."

The message had just arrived for a representative from Clan Scott to appear at Theffield Castle at once. Presumably Douglas was already on his way, and whether it was the warden or the earl who had requested their presence, it hardly mattered.

They could not deny Douglas.

If it were the earl . . . it meant he knew.

"Gillian is not as far along as—"

"No," Aidan said again, this time as firmly as if his brother were not his chief. "I met with him before and will do so again. Gillian needs you here."

Graeme watched him as he continued to pace back and forth. "If Theffield suspects . . . you will not admit to having her."

"Nay, I will not. Clarissa is convinced he will never accept me.

But if Douglas hears the merest suggestion of it, he'll ask questions."

"We will not lie to the warden."

"Neither will I give her back."

He stopped, waiting for his brother's reaction. But Graeme simply frowned. "Of course you will not. Your stance is mine, though do not expect Douglas to acquiesce if it comes to that."

"Thank you, brother."

The words hardly seemed adequate, but he could think of no others. Graeme had no allegiance to her, but his support had been unwavering.

"Do not thank me until the meeting ends in success. If all goes well and Theffield delivers on his promise to remove Caxton, we will devise a plan then."

"A few more days . . ."

"A few more days, and the fate of the borderlands will be decided."

He should let her go—and well he knew it. If he simply let her go, she would be safe. Their clan would be safe. But as he walked from Graeme's chamber, he remembered the empty feeling of sitting outside the gates of Dunburg Abbey, thinking Clarissa had but moments left with him.

He could never do it.

He could not let her go.

Aidan found Malcolm in the hall playing dice. Graeme had insisted he take an escort from Highgate End to Bowden Castle, even though the ride was short. He smiled in anticipation of how Lawrence would react to being awoken for yet another journey across the border, his presence having been specifically requested by Douglas.

"We leave for Theffield Castle," he said to Malcolm as he and his dice partners stood to greet him.

"Theffield?" Malcolm nodded toward the others in parting and followed him out of the hall. "At this hour?"

"Aye," he said, making his way toward the kitchens. "Douglas himself requested my presence."

Malcolm stopped and it took Aidan a moment to realize his man was no longer following him.

"Is it wise to go there, given the circumstances?" Malcolm asked when Aidan turned back to him.

"The circumstances?"

The hair on his arms stood straight as he waited for Malcolm's explanation. He knew, of course, what he meant, but there was no way he could—

"His daughter," he confirmed with a glance toward the Prison Tower. "Does the earl know Lady Clarissa—"

Aidan advanced on Malcolm so quickly that he actually took a step back.

"How," he ground out, "do you know about that?"

Malcom had not known why he'd been sent to fetch Father Simon.

Fear, the kind he'd only experienced a few times in his life, crept up his back and laid claim to every bone in his body. They'd told no one of her presence save Gillian, Fiona, Morgan, and Lewis. Not one of them would have uttered a word of Clarissa's presence here. And if someone had chanced to see them the night they'd gone to the river, none would have known her identity.

"Malcolm?"

"A rumor, 'tis all. One Donnon heard from a servant he met on the road who'd come from Sutworth. But none would dare—"

"Goddammit."

Theffield knew.

Cursing, he looked toward the tower where Clarissa waited for him to return as he'd promised to do after speaking to Graeme.

She couldn't stay here. Theffield likely planned to send men here to search for her after he lured Aidan across the border. He could ask Allie and Reid to hide her, but there was no time to go to Brockburg, the opposite direction of Theffield Castle.

He didn't need to think on it any longer. There was one place she would be safe. One family that would take her in, without question, and luckily, he'd been heading there already, though he was unsure why Douglas specifically requested Lawrence's presence.

THE POOR STEWARD had appeared confused, but he'd gone to fetch Lawrence nonetheless. Aidan had known the steward since he was old enough to ride to Bowden Castle, and he and Lawrence had gotten themselves into plenty of questionable situations before.

This would certainly qualify as the most questionable of them all.

"Let me guess," Lawrence said as he stepped out into the night, stretching his mouth wide in a yawn. "My good friend Aidan de Sowlis and his lovely Lady Clarissa."

With her hood pulled down over her brow, it was impossible to see her face. Even when she looked up at Lawrence, only her chin and cheeks were visible.

And her lips.

Aidan should be thinking of many things, but he certainly should not be thinking of Clarissa's lips.

"'Tis good to see you again," she said to his friend, her words barely loud enough for them to hear.

"And you, my lady." Lawrence lifted his brows, waiting.

"Not here," Aidan whispered, pulling them into an alcove not far from where they stood.

"We need your help," he said.

"Then it is yours."

Aidan looked down at his thumb before even realizing he'd

done so. Lawrence must have seen him, because he lifted his own thumb.

Lawrence laughed and glanced at Clarissa. "How old were we, ten and one?"

"Ten and two."

"And convinced our older brothers both thought us children."

"Aye, because we were children," Aidan said.

"And younger brothers both." Lawrence smiled at Clarissa. "And so we decided to become blood brothers, and promised never to treat each other as mere 'youngins,' the word my own brother used to describe us. I despised the word and all of the trappings that came along with being second—"

"Blood brothers?" Clarissa interrupted. But then she seemed to notice Lawrence's thumb still hovering in the air. "Do not tell me you—"

"We did," Aidan assured her. "Which is why I ask now," his voice turned serious, "for your family to take her in. We have reason to believe—"

"'Tis done."

When Lawrence held out his hand to Clarissa, Aidan's chest swelled with pride. He could not have chosen a better brother, with the exception of the one he'd been born with.

"I will explain on the way to Theffield."

About to lead Clarissa into the keep, Lawrence laughed aloud. Luckily, none but the three of them were there to hear it.

"It seems my friend does not want me to get much sleep," he said. "His nighttime jaunts have become more and more common of late."

Aidan found himself grinning as he followed the pair back toward the keep's entrance.

"I fear it is my fault," she said.

"If I faulted you for anything," Lawrence said, "it would be for choosing him"—he nodded his head back toward Aidan—"rather than a real chief's second son. A man worthy of such a woman—"

"That's enough," Aidan said, knowing his friend did indeed have a reputation with women to uphold. Or at least, Lawrence thought he did.

Though he couldn't see Clarissa's face, Aidan could imagine her sad smile when she said, "A woman whose very presence has become more of a burden than she would like."

He was about to respond when his friend did so for him. "Your father is a burden on *you*—and so are his cruel interventions to a matter that should have been put to rest long ago."

Lawrence turned back toward him, his sly smile making Aidan groan in anticipation of the words he was about to utter.

"I knew you would not let her go," he said. "And now we will show Lord Theffield exactly what it means to be the second son of a Scots chief."

Despite the dire situation they'd found themselves in this night, Aidan could not help but smile at his friend's words. He'd always said a second son was the fiercest of them all, for he was freed of the expectations that weighed down the firstborn. And though he did not quite believe it to be true, the knowledge that Clarissa was safe, for a time, and that Lawrence would be by his side, come what may, Aidan breathed a bit easier.

If they walked into a trap of Theffield's making, then it would be up to them to find a way out.

CHAPTER 18

"*W*here is she?"

Aidan ignored Douglas, who glared at him from the corner of the room. Theffield had deliberately kept them from speaking alone, so the warden knew only what the earl had told him—that unless Clan Scott confessed to hiding his daughter from him and revealed her whereabouts, they were at an impasse.

Knowing he risked raising the earl's ire, Aidan nonetheless refused to give him what he desired.

"The same day you left Theffield Castle, after calling upon my good graces to assist you—"

"You were willing to do nothing more than stall our progress."

Though he said the words, Aidan did not share Clarissa's confidence that her father had never intended to help them. But it was the only move they had left, and so he would make it.

"How dare you question my honor," the earl snarled.

Aidan did not back down. "How dare *you* accuse me of kidnapping your daughter."

"Enough!"

Douglas had not become Lord Warden of the Scottish

Marches by keeping quiet. Men feared him, but unlike Theffield, most respected him too.

"You've accused de Sowlis of hiding your daughter, and refuse to treat with us until he relents. I believe it's time for you to explain yourself."

Even the earl was not immune to Douglas's powers of persuasion. Though the man clearly did not appreciate being given an order, he answered Douglas despite it.

"As you may have heard," Theffield said, his eyes never leaving Aidan, "my daughter's marriage to Lord Stanley was recently annulled."

Though Aidan had known about the annulment, of course, hearing it said aloud gave Aidan nearly as much pleasure as reaching across the wooden table and punching the earl in the face would have. He'd thought of that punch, and the pleasure it would give him, from the moment he entered the keep. Only his memory of his father's lecture on what it meant to be a guest in another's home, even an enemy's home, had given him the strength to restrain himself.

And, of course, Douglas. Aidan did value his own life, after all.

"She returned to Theffield but has since—" he cleared his throat, "—gone missing."

Aidan could feel Douglas looking at him, but he did not meet the man's gaze. Instead, he watched the earl as closely as if Clarissa's life depended on it.

Because it very well might.

"And you believe de Sowlis to be involved?"

"I know he is," Theffield insisted, but he blinked just before he made the bold accusation.

He was lying.

Theffield may *think* he was involved in Clarissa's disappearance, but he did not know for certain.

"De Sowlis?"

He would rectify his sin later. But for now, lying to Douglas may very well be the difference between keeping, or losing, Theffield's support.

"I had nothing to do with his daughter's disappearance," he said, his voice firm. Turning to the earl, he said, "Putting our tenuous alliance in jeopardy would not be in the best interest of my clan."

Theffield's eyes narrowed. The earl did not believe him.

"We shall see."

And then the brute smiled.

Aidan thanked whichever saint had led Malcolm to reveal what he knew of Clarissa's stay at Highgate End. For if he'd not admitted as much, she would still be there when Theffield's men arrived to search the castle. Graeme could refuse them, of course, but doing so would not relieve the earl's suspicion.

As if reading his thoughts, Theffield said, "My men are likely already discovering the truth, or mistruth, of your words."

Just as he'd suspected. But Aidan played along with the Englishman who thought he was so damn clever. "Your men?"

Theffield stood so abruptly the chair nearly toppled behind him. "The men I have dispatched to Highgate End," he declared triumphantly. "If they find her, I will have you arrested."

"And when they do not?" Aidan asked, standing.

Theffield's head twitched from him to Douglas and back.

You should be nervous, you traitorous—

"If your men do not discover what you believe they will find at Highgate End?" Douglas prompted, sounding like a human version of the wild boar from which his nickname was derived. The man even had an inn named after him.

Theffield's jaw twitched before that same cruel smile spread across his face again. He was so certain of his victory.

"If Clan Scott is proven innocent," he said, "then I shall order Caxton to relinquish his position as warden, providing the terms de Sowlis set forth still stand."

"They do." Douglas nodded—a courtesy he then undermined

by walking from the room before the earl, an indication that he refused to defer to the man as a superior despite his title. "You will find us at the inn in your village," he added, another slight against the earl.

Neither man spoke as they were escorted from the keep. Only after they'd mounted and ridden far beyond the outer walls, their men riding behind them, did the warden speak to him again. "And now, de Sowlis, I will have the truth."

"The truth will have to wait."

If Douglas hadn't heard what he did—the distant pounding of horses' hooves—Aidan would have been in for a blistering retort. Instead, Douglas held his hand in the air, summoning the other four men who accompanied him to surround their chief as he turned to face the threat. Without discussing it, Aidan rode to the front and Lawrence to the back.

And they waited.

He spotted the gold and red banners first. His shoulders relaxing, Aidan continued to grip the handle of his dirk just in case. As the horses came closer, it became clear they were, indeed, Theffield's men. He turned to indicate as much to those behind him.

The man at the front of the group, Theffield's sergeant in all likelihood, spotted them first. He slowed as Aidan counted nine mounted knights.

"Greetings," he called, ignoring the look of contempt on the leader's face.

"Scots" was his only answer.

The fact that they had accepted Clarissa so easily was a testament to her standing with Clan Scott. She was one of them now, and he'd made sure Lawrence knew the lass was under his protection.

These men, on the other hand, were decidedly not.

"My friend offers a kindly welcome," Lawrence spat. "You could do the same."

"Or perhaps your master has yet to teach you proper manners," Douglas growled.

For a man who spent his days negotiating peace, his temper had not diminished a whit. Between him and Lawrence, they would be lucky to leave Theffield with their heads on their shoulders.

The sergeant drew his sword at Douglas's words. Aidan took his own off his dagger and put both hands into the air. The last thing he wanted was for a war with Theffield to begin here, on the man's own property.

"We are under the protection of your master," Douglas said. "Allow us to pass and no further exchange is necessary."

"And put down your sword while you do it," Lawrence muttered, luckily not loud enough for anyone but Aidan to hear him.

Though he looked as if he wished to argue, Theffield's sergeant finally lowered his sword. Looking at them as if they were not good enough to clean the mud from his horse's hooves, his eyes narrowed.

Finally, he kicked the side of his mount so hard the beast let out a weary protest. Aidan didn't wonder at the rough treatment. Most men emulated their leader, and theirs was the worst sort of bastard, a man who cared for nothing save himself.

Had he dared hope the distraction might make Douglas forget his question, the look the older man gave him as they once again rode away from Theffield Castle told him otherwise.

"I'll have that explanation now, de Sowlis."

Lawrence grinned at him and then rode ahead, leaving him alone with the warden.

Traitor.

"And likely that is why Theffield requested Derrickson."

Grateful for the temporary reprieve, Aidan looked ahead toward his friend.

"We thought the request was yours."

Douglas huffed. "This dispute between Clan Karyn and the Earl of Rockford does not

aid matters. I fear if we avoid war this time, their feud may throw us right back to where we started. Theffield knows that."

And thought to instigate, to complicate the matter. He truly was the worst sort of bastard.

"Explain."

So much for his reprieve. "I lied to Theffield," he said, looking straight ahead. "Lady Clarissa is safe, though not at Highgate End, thankfully."

He was rewarded with the exact response he'd expected.

"Do you aim to start a war, then?"

Aidan navigated an overgrowth of fireweed as the dry weather as he considered how to answer the man. As young men, both he and Graeme had been terrified of the clan chief, their father's closest friend, even though they'd known him since childhood. As a grown man and warrior, Aidan would like to think he was less intimidated by the man, but the truth was, the king had made an excellent choice when he'd chosen Douglas as Lord Warden.

"Nay, not apurpose."

He did look at Douglas then. "When she appealed to Lawrence and me to help her escape her father—"

"The man who holds full jurisdiction over her—"

"Held. She is now under the protection of Clan Scott."

Douglas would kill him yet.

"At the time, the annulment had not yet been granted. I planned to leave her at Sutworth, where the lady could appeal to Dunburg Abbey—"

"A nun?" he growled. "She cannot—"

"She has the gold necessary," he said, but before Douglas could respond, he added, "but Dunburg lost their benefactor. And so she had nowhere to go—"

"With the exception of Theffield Castle?"

Douglas was angry, and Aidan didn't blame him. The situation was less than ideal for any of them.

"Her father is a traitorous bastard who—"

"Is her father."

Aidan had no choice now. He took a deep breath, slowed his mount to a stop, and waited for Douglas to do the same. As the men behind them followed suit, Aidan attempted to keep himself as steady as possible so Douglas could look him in the eye and understand his position.

"And I will be her husband."

The decision was made. Had been made well before today. Clarissa might be willing to sacrifice herself for a perceived greater good, but he refused to let her. He would not abandon the woman he loved. Ever again.

"Goddammit, de Sowlis. Do you understand what you've done?"

"Aye, sire. I understand it well. I've fallen in love with a woman who has endured shameful mistreatment from not one but two men who put their greed and selfish desires above her well-being. I understand that by doing so, I've put my family, my clan, and our allies in jeopardy. And were my father with us now—" he prayed his father was watching, and listening, because God knew Aidan needed every bit of support he could muster, "—he would curse me for a fool. But he would also honor the pledge I've made. A pledge my brother, the chief of our clan, has seconded."

Aidan could not make his position clearer. Clan Scott would not waver in this. She was as good as one of them, if not yet in name.

"Where is she?"

Lawrence, who had ridden back to join them, spoke up. "With my family."

He could have said she was at Bowden Castle. But he had not. Aidan tried not to smile at his friend's choice of words, which had effectively declared Clan Karyn's position on the matter.

Douglas looked between the men, his cheeks red, and then indicated they should keep moving. He didn't speak for a time. And though doubt attempted to creep into his mind, Aidan stopped it. The decision had been made. Mayhap he'd been foolish, but his father had taught them another lesson, one he'd taken to heart.

Doubt was a poison that would eat away at you until none of your convictions remained.

"Theffield will kill you when he finds out what you've done," Douglas said finally.

"He is welcome to try. As long as he does so after the new English warden has been chosen."

Either way, the outcome would be decided soon enough.

CHAPTER 19

*A*idan was back.

Though no one told her as much, she'd been summoned from her room without explanation, and Clarissa had only left the main keep of Bowden Castle twice in the time she'd stayed here. Once, Lawrence's sister, one of the loveliest women she'd ever met with the exception of Lady Gillian, had snuck her out late at night. She'd tried to tell the other woman it was not safe, but she'd refused to listen. They only went as far as the interior garden, but Clarissa could not have been more grateful for the reprieve.

Then yesterday, five full nights after she first arrived, she had been startled by a visit from Lawrence's father, the chief of Clan Karyn. When he ordered her to walk with him, she had not thought to argue. His gruff manners made her uncomfortable at first, but by the time the chief returned Clarissa to her chamber, she was smiling easily, if not often. Though he was kind to her, even after admitting to his dislike of "everything English," Clarissa could understand the purpose of his visit.

He never said as much, but he clearly worried her presence may cause exactly the kind of trouble Aidan hoped to avoid. His carefully worded questions and looks of concern told her what everyone else denied—Clarissa could start a war.

Or at the very least, prevent one from being avoided.

She should never have asked Aidan to escort her north. It had been the kind of selfish act her father would have committed without self-recrimination. But Clarissa was most certainly not her father.

As she followed the servant from her temporary chamber, through a long corridor and out of a side entrance that led directly to the stables, Clarissa's pulse began to race. She'd thought of little else besides Aidan these past days, and despite the unease that continued to plague her, the voice in her head that insisted she could not stay with him, Clarissa could not deny the rush of pleasure at the thought of seeing him again.

His back was turned toward her.

Aidan held the reins of both their mounts as he looked off into the distance. Framed by the waning light of day, he appeared every bit the warrior. The sight reminded her of what it had been like to see him on the jousting field after all those years apart. Aidan had sat tall and proud atop his horse, looking into the temporary stands surrounding the field. The excitement of being there had not yet worn off, and she could hardly take in the sights and smells—not all of them pleasant—when he looked at her and everything around her fell away.

"My sister will be sorry she did not see you off."

She turned, the deep voice from behind startling her out of her reverie. Lawrence walked toward her, grinning at his friend beyond her.

"The great Aidan de Sowlis, taken unaware by a wee slip of a woman."

When her gaze returned to Aidan, she understood what Lawrence had meant. She'd caught him off guard. He had not noticed her standing there, behind him.

"Come," Aidan said to her, reaching for her. When he took her hand, she wanted to squeeze and never let go. But he helped her onto the horse, and all too soon, a cool slip of leather replaced his strong warmth. She watched him mount his own horse in one effortless movement, unable to look away, and then realized she had not yet answered Lawrence's comment.

"Please tell her the pleasure was mine," she said.

"Until we meet again, my lady."

Clarissa laughed at Lawrence's wink, wondering how many ladies he had seduced with that gesture. She'd overheard enough to know Aidan's friend had something of a reputation.

Did Aidan as well?

Remembering the last time they were alone together, she avoided looking directly at him as they rode side by side back to Highgate End. When she finally did glance his way, Aidan's head was tilted up toward the sky.

She hadn't noticed it before, but it seemed just a bit darker than it had a moment before. The air felt heavier too.

"Will we make it to Highgate before the storm?"

In answer, the wind rustled through the trees like crumpled parchment.

"Nay, lass. We will not."

The sun dipped behind thick gray clouds. Aidan left the path, and Clarissa followed without question. The long sleeves of her simple deep green riding gown kept out the chill that accompanied the quick change in weather. But if it began to rain, an inevitability if the distant rumbling was any indication, they were in for an uncomfortable ride back.

"Hurry," he said, riding in front of her on a trail that became more and more overgrown as they followed it. Trees surrounded them. She would have asked where they were going, but a loud crack in the sky prevented her from doing so.

In truth, Clarissa was not alarmed. She loved the rain. Loved hearing it patter or pound on the roof as she watched the fat droplets from her window. Loved the feel of it against her skin.

It had been dry as of late, but people usually complained about inclement weather, for any number of reasons. She secretly reveled in the wildness of it. Even now, with the possibility of a soaking very real, she could not drum up much enthusiasm for disappointment.

Another, much louder crack in the air startled her horse. It was decidedly more calming to watch a rainstorm from afar than it was to be in the thick of one.

"Oh!"

The ruins in front of them seemed to appear from out of nowhere. A three-sided structure with only a portion of its roof intact presided over a large ditch and another, lower set of ruins.

"What is it?" she asked, dismounting behind Aidan, aware of his sense of urgency.

"An old Roman fort," he said, leading their mounts to an open area on the opposite side of the structure. Just as he returned, the first fat drops of rain fell from the sky, and Clarissa did not have to be told where to go. She ran past the ditch and into the only area with a roof. Aidan dove in after her.

As if it had only been waiting for them to find shelter, the sky opened with another loud crack.

The ditch in front of them began to fill as water sluiced from above. Clarissa looked at the puddles and then up as far as she could see from beneath their tenuous shelter. The roof seemed in danger of crumbling at any moment.

Finally, with nothing left to explore, she turned toward him.

Aidan either knew this place well or had no interest in examining it further, for he was already staring at her. Staring in a way that sent her heart straight to her throat. Was he thinking of the intimacies they'd shared? Of his hands on her breasts or—

"I missed you."

She hadn't expected that, not from the hungry way he was looking at her. But she couldn't tell him about the ache of longing that had threatened to consume her while he was away. It would only make it harder . . . later.

"How was the meeting with my father?" Clarissa folded her fingers together in front of her, hoping it would keep them from touching him.

"Not well. He suspects that I am hiding you."

Clarissa's fingers flew apart. "Did he say as much? Did he accuse you—"

"I should start from the beginning."

Listening to his account of the meeting, Clarissa became more and more agitated. They had *searched* Highgate Castle? She had come so close to being caught. Perhaps it would have been for the best had her father found her.

"Did you hear me?"

Indeed, she had not.

"I'm sorry. I just—"

Clarissa stumbled backward and sat on the crumbling stone bench behind her. Though it, like the entire structure, was beyond repair, enough of the original bench remained to give her a dry seat. Aidan claimed it was safe to return, that her father's men found nothing, of course, and were long gone. That her father would be beholden to remove Caxton from power, just as he'd promised. They expected to receive word of the warden's replacement any day. And when that happened, when a new warden was appointed—

"Clarissa?" He sat next to her, the rain continuing to fall around them, and took her hands in his. "I will not allow him to harm you."

She knew she should pull away. She could not bear to. Instead, she shook her head. "Aidan, you do not understand my father. He will not rest until I am discovered."

"So be it."

Her eyes widened.

"Douglas knows our position. Clan Scott—"

"Cannot do this!" Clarissa stood once again, breaking the contact she so desired. He did the same, standing just inches away from her.

"I know you, Aidan," she said. "You are the protector. Your responsibility is to the clan. If anything goes wrong," she swallowed, her throat raw, "you will blame me, and rightly so."

He reached for her again, cupping her face as if it were a fine piece of porcelain.

"You say my responsibility is to the clan. Clarissa, you are one of us. I offered my protection because I could never let anything happen to you. Marry me. Become my wife, and there will be no further questions about where you belong."

A single tear escaped, unbidden, as his hands branded her. She could no sooner escape their grasp than she could keep running. Nor did she want to. But still, this was not right.

"You would marry me to protect me?"

"I would marry you because I love you."

Oh God, Aidan. I love you too. But if I say the words, how could I ever leave you?

"He will come back for me."

Aidan's hands slid from her face to her shoulders. "Aye, he will."

"You will have made a new enemy."

His hands dropped down to her waist. "Perhaps."

"For certain. You put your clan at risk."

He pulled her toward him, then lifted her chin so he was looking into her eyes.

"Marry me, Clarissa."

Aidan would not be dissuaded. He was going to kiss her, and Clarissa desperately wanted him to. She'd thought about the feel of his lips on hers nearly every moment he was away. She wanted that, and more.

But he would have her answer first.

Nothing would give her greater pleasure than to say yes. To become the wife of this hardened warrior whose touch was so gentle that it made her forget every one of her troubles when she was in his arms.

"I . . . I cannot."

CHAPTER 20

"*W*hy?"

He pulled back just slightly but didn't let go. Aidan would never let her go again.

This time, he understood exactly what held her back.

"I've put your clan in too much danger already."

Aidan searched her eyes. He believed she meant it, but there was more to her hesitation. His Clarissa didn't truly believe she deserved happiness. The insidious words of her father and her former husband had lingered with her.

"Do you love me?"

"Aidan, I never intended—"

"Do you love me?"

He had laid himself as bare as a warrior venturing onto the battlefield without armor. But knowing the answer made it easier to ask the question.

At least, he thought he knew it. But as the silence stretched—

"Aye, I love you, Aidan," she said in a burst of words. "How could any woman not? But—"

He kissed her, not wasting another moment. As rain pounded the earth around them, water splashing in puddles around the walls of the old fort, he kissed her, roughly enough to make her forget any additional protests.

At least, that was his aim.

Though he ached to be inside her, to claim Clarissa as his for eternity, he would not do so. Not yet. But he was determined to make her scream his name loudly enough to wake the dead Roman soldiers who'd once graced these walls.

Luckily, the riding gown was not so tightly laced that it kept him from moving his lips to her neck, and lower. Though he could reach only the very tops of her full breasts, it was just enough to distract her from the touch he knew was foreign to her.

But it would not be for long.

In fact, she would become quite accustomed to his fingers, which had already lifted the layers of both gowns, ignoring their weight on his wrists. Navigating the shift as well, he found his target, or close to it.

He squeezed the soft skin of her inner thigh and smiled at her gasp. Continuing to twirl his tongue with hers, wishing he could wrap his lips around her nipple but not willing to stop, he dipped his hand closer to her core. Pushing aside the last remaining barrier, Aidan cupped her fully as he stood, wanting to see her expression.

Cheeks flushed, hair spilling around her in every direction, Clarissa looked as if she'd already been ravished.

Not quite yet.

He stilled his hand, waiting, until she finally pressed against it.

"I'm going to slip my fingers inside you," he said, "and hear my name from your lips before we're through."

The minx shrugged, actually shrugged, as if she doubted him.

Aidan was not fooled. She ruined the effect of her bravado by biting her lip. It was as good a place to start as any. He ran the tip of his tongue to the seam where her teeth met her poor lower lip, coaxing it to open. When it did, he plunged inside.

And his fingers followed.

She was dripping wet and more than ready to come apart at his touch, so Aidan circled and pressed with his fingers, unrelenting, even when Clarissa tried to pull her mouth away. If the sensations were too much, she would simply have to learn to be overwhelmed by them.

Aidan did not relent, not in anything, and certainly not in her pleasure.

Devouring her mouth as he slowed the pace down below, he captured her low groan. Hard and more than ready to sink himself into her, Aidan relied on years of discipline to ignore the powerful urge to claim this woman as his own. Instead, he continued his gentle assault until Clarissa met his pace, her hips circling and pressing against his hand.

Only when he felt a very slight tremor beneath his fingers did he relent. Pulling his mouth from hers, he watched in amazed delight as her angel's face was transformed by passion—lips wide apart and head tilted back. When she finally found release, the powerful spasms gripping his fingers, he waited . . .

And was finally rewarded.

"Aidan!" she called, squeezing her eyes shut. "Oh my."

Her chest heaved up and down, and Aidan tried to resist the urge to reach into the neckline of her gown. Actually, he did not try very hard. Slipping his thumb down as far is it would reach, he quickly realized he needed assistance. Reaching his other hand out from under the folds of her double-layered gown, he used it to pull down the offending material. Already loosened, it gave way just enough for him to uncover the prize he sought. There were too many folds of fabric to expose her entire breast . . . but it was enough.

Wrapping his lips around her, Aidan suddenly wanted nothing more than to ensure Clarissa found release again. Every time she thought to leave him, to spare his clan and sacrifice herself for their safety, he wanted her to think of this moment. Every time the rain began to fall or Clarissa heard the loud crack of thunder in the sky, he wanted her to clench tight in memory of his hands caressing that most intimate part of her. He wanted the nipples on her breasts to peak as they did now under his ministrations.

"Again," he murmured against her. "Come again for me, my love."

Pulling down the fabric from Clarissa's other breast, caressing every bit of skin he could find, Aidan used his thumb and the very tip of his tongue to give both breasts the attention they deserved. Clarissa's quick breaths confirmed what her clenched fingers on his back told him . . . she was close.

Aidan did not let up, and when she grabbed a fistful of his hair, Aidan's moan entangled with hers until the cry he so coveted was forced from her lips. He captured it, his mouth covering hers as possessively as was acceptable.

When he finally pulled away, he amended his earlier assessment.

Now she looked thoroughly ravished.

"A small taste of what awaits my wife in the days ahead."

She sighed, a defeated sound that should have saddened him. After all, it was the first time he'd ever asked a woman to marry him. An enthusiastic yes would have been ideal, but Aidan would take her sigh, accompanied by a small smile, instead.

Glancing out of their makeshift shelter, he realized the rain had stopped. Neither of them had noticed. He set her gown to rights, and forced himself to step back. "We should be getting back—"

"To Highgate End?"

"Aye, love."

"Do you think it's safe?"

"I do. The deal is done. We'll be watching for your father's men now, just in case, so he cannot surprise us again. And by the time he learns you're really here, Caxton will be replaced . . . and you will be my wife."

He waited for her to argue, but Clarissa surprised him. She

came to him instead, placing her small hands on his cheeks.

"I love you, Aidan de Sowlis."

And though his chest swelled to hear it, those were not the words he waited for.

"And I love you, lass. But as to the other—will you be my wife?"

Lifting herself up to him, Clarissa closed her eyes and touched her lips to his. He resisted turning the innocent kiss into something more.

"Nothing would give me greater pleasure."

As they rode through the gates of Highgate Castle, Clarissa thought of their last moments together at the fort. She listened as Aidan told her the history of how this wall had been erected, and then abandoned, by the Romans. The ditch, he said, had once been a bath house. And though the tale was fascinating, Clarissa could think only of one thing.

She had not lied to him.

Nothing would give her greater pleasure than becoming Aidan's wife . . . but she could not do it. To accept such an offer knowing she would be responsible for the strife that would ensue . . .

He'd never listen to her. She could see the stubborn determination in his eyes. Oh, how she loved him, but his unwavering loyalty to her could lead to a lifetime of battles between Clan Scott and the Earl of Theffield.

"Nay, lass. Not the tower."

They'd dismounted and Clarissa had assumed—

"You will not be locked away any longer. But 'tis your choice if you would like to stay there or in the main keep."

"Do you think that's wise? People will talk—"

"And we will tell them. We are to be married, Clarissa. I will not have you—"

This time, it was her turn to display a bit of stubbornness.

"Nay," she said, shaking her head and walking toward the Prison Tower. "Until Caxton is removed—"

"Which will happen any day. In the meantime—"

"In the meantime, listen to the lady."

Graeme had approached them from behind.

"It took you long enough, brother."

She'd been too wrapped up in Aidan to notice Graeme's approach. The realization brought on another one—their position was too exposed. Though it appeared to be mealtime, the court-yard emptier than normal, anyone could see them. Clarissa had, out of habit, donned her cape and lifted the hood over her head, but would that truly prevent her from being exposed?

"Might we have this discussion in a more private place?" she asked.

Both men looked at her then, as if surprised she was the one who'd made such an argument, but they relented. As they followed her closer to the west wall, a lone guard on the parapets above their heads, Clarissa took charge.

"I will remain in there—" she gestured toward the tower, "— until Caxton is removed."

Graeme's eyes widened. "So it is done?"

Aidan scowled at her and then explained to his brother every-thing that had happened. Graeme had surmised some of the story already. Her father's men had appeared at Highgate End a few days prior, demanding to search both the castle and the grounds. Graeme had easily acquiesced, much to the ire of his officers, who would have denied them.

"They were none too happy with the outcome," Graeme said with a smile.

"English bastards," Aidan said, and then to her, "Sorry, love."

The endearment, so easily given, stung. If she left, it would hurt Aidan. Again. He would be devastated, though no less so than she.

"I best be more careful as we'll be having another English-woman reside permanently at Highgate End."

Graeme looked back and forth between them, and then smiling, he clasped Aidan's hand and pulled him toward him. She watched the brothers embrace, suddenly torn.

"Welcome to Clan Scott," Graeme said to her then. "Gillian will be so happy to hear the news."

"How does she fare?" Clarissa asked.

"My lady is well. The sickness seems to have passed."

"I am overjoyed to hear it." She wouldn't wish the feelings Gillian had described to her on anyone. Well, maybe her father. And Stanley.

She was uncharitable to think such a thing.

"You must be tired, Lady Clarissa."

"Clarissa, please."

Graeme bowed, an odd gesture for the chief. "And you will call me Graeme."

Very few used the clan chief's given name, and she was honored he'd given her leave to do so. It was almost as if . . . as if he were truly happy to welcome her to his family.

But how could that be?

Aidan took her hand and squeezed it before releasing it. "Come to the hall—"

"Nay, Aidan. I cannot. Not yet."

Maybe never.

Aidan looked to his brother for support, but when Graeme merely shrugged, he finally admitted defeat. "I will bring you a tray—"

"Nay, you will enjoy a meal with your family and have one sent to me," she countered. "I could use a rest after our quite interesting journey back."

She felt the heat begin in her neck and rise to her face. She hadn't meant to say . . .

"Interesting, " Graeme said good-naturedly. "Not a word I'd normally use—"

"Graeme," Aidan interjected who grinned at her unintended gaffe.

"I meant to say—"

"No need," Graeme interrupted. "I already understood what you meant." Still grinning, he said to Aidan, "We have much to discuss, brother. Perhaps you could take your lady for a late-night bath in the river another night."

Clarissa felt her jaw drop open. She wanted to accuse Aidan of sharing their secret, but he appeared as surprised as she felt.

His older brother winked at her, reminding her of Lawrence. "Nothing happens at Highgate End that I do not know about," he said to them both.

And then Graeme looked at her, his smile slipping, and she realized the truth of his words. He knew. Somehow, Aidan's brother knew, or guessed, what she planned.

Graeme knew she was planning to leave.

CHAPTER 21

*E*ventually, she fell asleep, thinking of Aidan, Graeme and Gillian in the hall, eating and drinking and sharing stories. Planning for the possible war that she had helped bring about. Only to be awoken by light streaming into her chamber from four arrow slits. Even though it was still early, the bright rays illuminated the otherwise dark chamber, promising a new beginning.

She could allow herself to dream, could she not?

Aye, and why not. She envisioned what it would be like if she answered Aidan "aye." She saw herself sitting beside him, laughing at another of his jests and sharing a meal with him. She imagined another scene, one of her standing beside Gillian as she birthed her first babe, a niece or nephew. And then another, this one very different from the other two. She and Aidan were in a bedchamber much like this one, only bigger. He stood next to her, his hand under her gown. She closed her eyes, remembering keenly each and every stroke. His lips, both soft and hard at the same time, moving against hers as he lifted her higher and higher yet, to a place she never would have found without him.

"A small taste of what awaits my wife in the days ahead."

She let her mind flit to another vision. This time they were by the river. Their bodies touched as he explored her most intimate spot, and she, bold enough to do the same, learned to please him as well.

Clarissa sighed aloud, the lonely sound echoing in her small chamber. That future could be hers if she were bold enough to take it. A man who loved her, who did not believe her to be unworthy, wished to take her to wife.

What was the alternative? They'd not yet heard from Father Simon. She couldn't very well go wandering about the countryside, alone, looking for the nearest convent, hoping they would accept her without a sponsor. Even if such a thing were possible, the thought of living out her life without Aidan, without ever knowing his touch again . . .

She feared it would kill her. And Aidan too.

Well, as Eda had always told her, lying in bed would certainly not help. When she rose from the bed to dress, Clarissa startled at the sight in front of her. A large wooden tray with freshly baked bread and an array of fruit sat waiting on the table. Had Morgan been here already?

After eating a handful of grapes while she dressed, Clarissa gathered up the cuts of bread with her and headed to the only place she felt safe in Highgate End. The bakehouse. As she entered the building through the underground corridor, Clarissa took a bite of the bread she carried, the small mutiny an answer to her training to never walk while eating.

"Good morn, Lewis."

The gray-haired baker stood at the oven with his back to her. Though warm inside the bakehouse, the smell of freshly baked bread more than compensated for the small inconvenience.

"And to you, my lady," he said, pulling out what looked like trenchers. As Lewis had told her the last time she visited him, he typically baked for the evening meal every morn. Occasionally, he provided special breads to the villagers, but much of his time was spent baking for those who lived here at Highgate Castle.

Theffield did not have its own baker. Her father thought the expense unnecessary, and so their cook did all of the baking as well.

"Tell me what to do," she said, waiting for Lewis's argument. Though she did not want to sit idle, he had stubbornly refused to give her a job on her past visits. "A lady should not work in the kitchens," he'd said. Perhaps not, but this lady desired the choice to do as she wished. So, hoping it would spur him into action, Clarissa picked up a bag of flour.

"Shall I dump this onto the table to make dough?"

"Nay, lass!" He pointed to a waiting bowl. "There. Knead that dough, if you please."

Poor Lewis. She did as he instructed, though not until she finished eating the bread she'd brought with her. Perhaps it was unladylike to do so, but she could not bring herself to care overly much.

"My lord found you, did he?"

Lewis had turned his back to the oven once again.

"Found me?" she asked, tipping the dough onto the table beneath it. Was he speaking of Graeme?

"Master Aidan. He brought you that bread you were eating, no?"

She'd just begun to knead the dough, but his words stopped her short. "Oh. Aidan brought that to me?"

"Aye, who else? Did you not speak to him then?"

"Nay," she said, her hands resuming their ministrations. "He must have left that tray for me while I was asleep."

"Forgive my impertinence, my lady, but it would not surprise me that he should do such a thing. Most men of his station would not serve those under him, serve a woman, if you'll forgive me for saying so. But it is not so with Aidan."

"Why do you say so?"

Lewis wiped his hands on his tunic and reached for the dough she'd finished kneading. Handing it to him, she watched in fascination as he quickly formed the sticky mass into what would become another trencher for the midday or evening meal.

"When his mother was ill, God rest her soul, my lord refused to leave her chamber. All of us were deeply affected when she passed, but none more so than he. There is no man kinder, or more loyal." Lewis, who'd already finished shaping the trencher, started to move each of his creations to the stone that sat in front of the large, fire-stoked oven.

"There was no need to be a seer like my sister to know he'd find someone to love."

Love.

"A seer?"

Lewis had a sister? Clarissa knew his wife was Highgate's alewife, but she'd not heard of a sister.

"She fancies herself one," he said, placing the last piece of dough near the oven. "But can hardly see the grass in front of her feet."

Lewis laughed at his own jest. She could not help but chuckle as well as she awaited the answer to her question.

"Or it could be this ol' man just knows the way of things."

Something told her he was being coy.

"Lewis?"

He shrugged, pulling a large sack of flour toward him.

"Or it could be that when we first met, I could see the truth in his eyes. And yours."

Everything Lewis said was true. Aidan truly was the kindest man alive, and she could not be the one to break his heart. Enough running. Enough hiding. Clarissa was ready to claim her place in this clan.

AIDAN KNOCKED at Clarissa's door, glancing at the man who stood beside him. Tall and lean, he was not much older than Graeme, though his experiences lent him an undeniable air of knowledge. Aidan had known Father Simon for as long as the man had been at Brockburg, back when his brother was betrothed to Catrina Kerr. From allies to enemies to allies once again, Clan Scott and Clan Kerr had a generations-long history, which had seen their families through the devastating loss of both chiefs, the unfortunate accident in battle that had ended their alliance and, more recently, a renewed friendship.

"Aidan? I'm glad you're here, I've something—"

She noticed Father Simon then, their unexpected guest bowing his head in deference to her, as befitted her station as an earl's daughter, even though such a gesture was not necessary. A more affable, tolerant, and intelligent man could not be found in all of Scotland, which was the precise reason Aidan had called on him for assistance.

"Oh!"

"Lady Clarissa, meet Father Simon of Brockburg. Father, may I present Lady Clarissa Harford, daughter of the Earl of Theffield."

Her curtsy was precise, that of an Englishwoman who had been trained her entire life to make such a greeting. She wore a gown Aidan had not seen before, a deep cranberry confection trimmed with gold around the low-hanging sleeves and neckline. A simple gold belt hung low on her hips. Her hair, as always, was pulled back partially on both sides away from her face with the majority of it falling down her back. Simple yet elegant, this was the lady who'd enchanted him. Though more refined than most, she lacked the air of superiority some in her station wore like a cloak.

"May we come inside?" he asked, and Clarissa immediately stepped aside.

The perfectly neat chamber smelled sweet, like its lady. A comfortable prison, but a prison nonetheless.

"Of course," she said, though they had already made their way inside. "I would offer you a seat . . ."

But there was one sole chair in the sparsely furnished room.

"No need," he said, changing his mind. Aidan had thought to leave her with Father Simon—to allow them to speak in private—but now he found his feet unable to move. Though Clarissa had agreed to stay at Highgate, to become his wife, he was no fool. His brother had confirmed earlier that day what he'd already suspected. Clarissa was as skittish as a hart knowing it was being hunted.

"I thought to send a message, but Lady Allie insisted on coming to speak with you," Father Simon said.

He could see Clarissa was confused and thought to explain. "I told you of my sister-in-law." Clarissa nodded. "She and her husband accompanied Father Simon here, though I've not seen them yet. Father has the reputation of being a somewhat reckless rider—"

"I arrived before them," Father boasted.

Aidan smiled at Brockburg's priest. "As for your vows against pride—"

"I took no such vow." He pretended to consider the matter further. "In fact, as I think on it, there may have been something . . ."

"Some say his time with the Kerr men has made Father—"

"I believe we are here to discuss Lady Clarissa."

The lady in question waited, hands folded in front of her. Aidan could not seem to look away from the twinkle of amusement in her eyes. Every day she spent away from Theffield, she became bolder, freer—more like the woman who'd boldly agreed to meet him at that lake than the one who'd looked up at him in fear in Theffield's courtyard, begging him to help her.

"Indeed," she said, looking at him. This look, no longer amused, was laced with the same desire he'd awoken feeling that morn, thinking of . . . well, things he should not be thinking of in front of the priest.

"Burness Abbey is a daughter house of Thrustan Abbey, no more than thirty miles north of here," Father Simon said. "Though it was built by King David and has received royal support for more than a hundred and fifty years, the Order of Cistercian nuns there have come upon difficult times of late."

Aidan had heard the tale already on their way to find Clarissa. He'd not yet told Father his assistance was no longer needed, as it was Clarissa's place to do so. His mother's words had guided him in this: *Speak for no one but yourself, and most especially not for a woman.* She'd said it so many times that even his stubborn father had begun to listen to her—no small feat given the chief's inclination had been to solve the problems of everyone around him. Even so, hearing Father's words aloud, watching her face as she realized what they implied . . .

Would she change her mind?

"They are eager to meet you," Father Simon finished. "And I am glad to take you there myself."

A heaviness settled in Aidan's stomach as he awaited her answer.

"I . . . this is quite unexpected," she began.

He couldn't do it.

Though the choice was hers, the thought of her accepting the priest's offer made him speak up.

"Your companions should have arrived by now," he interrupted. "Perhaps we should continue this conversation in the hall over a meal. When I received word of your arrival, supper was about to be served."

If Father Simon was startled by the abrupt change in agenda—Aidan was the one who'd suggested an immediate meeting with Clarissa—he covered it well. His good manners dictated he would accept the offer of a meal.

And he did.

"Very good," he said. "We shall discuss the particulars this evening—"

"And you will stay for the night, of course."

"Aye," Father said, confirming what Aidan already knew. The timing of the visit practically ensured it. But he simply could not shake the need to get Father Simon away from Clarissa.

"Come with us," he offered, certain she would decline. She'd remained in hiding these last days, at her own volition, after all.

"With pleasure."

He almost tripped over his own feet, his eyes darting to her face. Her shaky smile did not fool him. Clarissa was terrified, though he didn't know if it was Father Simon's offer that unsettled her or her decision to dine in the great hall.

What had changed her mind?

Dare he hope it was her acceptance of their situation? He knew Clarissa had spent the day with Lewis, and though he'd begun to make his way to the bakehouse not once but twice, he'd stopped himself both times. She'd always wished to learn how to bake, and he did not want to distract her from the experience— one she'd never been allowed before. So he spent the day training with his men, attempting not to think of her.

Attempting, but failing.

"Shall I send someone—"

"Nay, I am ready," she said, her shaky voice betraying her words.

Father Simon did not appear to notice. Aidan raised his hand, an indication for the priest to walk ahead, and then offered his arm to Clarissa. When she took it, slipping her hand through the crook of his elbow as he escorted her from the room, Aidan resisted the urge to pull her closer.

He smiled at the thought of how the others would react.

Lady Clarissa was about to be properly introduced to High-gate Castle.

CHAPTER 22

hey'd somehow avoided the discussion that Clarissa knew was necessary. She would tell Father Simon no, but she had not yet mustered the strength to do so. And so she ignored his inquisitive looks and attempted to enjoy her evening.

An easy feat while sitting between Gillian and Allie.

When they'd first walked through the doors of the great hall, a stunned silence had descended over the room. Clarissa had done her best to ignore the fuss by concentrating on the differences between the great halls in Theffield and Highgate—while the former was a place for the men to simply gather and eat each day, the latter was a warm, inviting space filled with laughter. Then Gillian and Allie whisked her into the fold, and she spent the rest of the meal listening to the two women tell stories of their time here at Highgate.

If they were trying to convince her it was a magical place from which no one would choose to leave, Clarissa needed no convincing. There was nowhere she would rather be than here, surrounded by love.

Aidan sat next to Allie's husband, but she darted glances at him throughout the meal. His eyes always seemed to be on her whenever she looked over.

Once, when she caught him staring, she lifted the corners of her lips in a smile meant to reassure him nothing had changed. If she'd thought for a brief moment Father Simon was the answer to her prayers, it was only because she doubted the sanity of her decision. Marrying Aidan was likely not the right thing to do. In fact, it felt utterly selfish. She found herself looking at Father Simon, wondering how much he knew. Did he suspect she had changed her mind?

Would he approve of their decision?

"She's not listening."

"When Reid was pursuing you, did you listen to anyone else when he was in the room? Even after I explicitly forbade you to even glance his way."

They were speaking to her. Or rather about her.

"You forbade Allie to speak to Reid?" she asked.

Allie grimaced, pushing away the trencher she shared with her husband.

"She did. Would you care to enlighten our guest with your recollection of when Highgate End hosted the council—"

"I remember the event well," Gillian said, turning to Clarissa. "I'd met Reid once before, at The Wild Boar, and he was, how shall I put this delicately—"

"A complete arse," the man in question interrupted.

Clearly he'd been listening to their conversation—with some amusement, it would seem. But when Clarissa attempted to look at him, she met Aidan's eyes instead.

"You're being kind," Gillian teased Reid. "I'd have used a stronger word, but it will do."

Allie sat back, lifting a cup of wine to her lips. She was clearly enjoying the memory, or at least her sister's retelling of it.

Gillian frowned. "I knew immediately she was attracted to him—"

"And still is."

"Reid," Gillian admonished. "Would you please allow me to finish?"

The rogue, for certainly that was the best word to describe him, lifted his mug in silent acquiescence.

"And I will admit to being a mite stubborn about his pursuit of my sister—"

"Or *her* pursuit of *me*," Reid said.

This time it was Allie who intervened, swatting her husband on the arm. In response, he pulled her toward him and kissed her. To imagine such a thing! In front of a room full of men . . . and the kiss was no small peck on the cheek. In fact, he stopped only when the banging of mugs and cheers became so loud they were impossible to ignore.

"As I was saying . . ." Gillian smiled. "I was convinced Reid was not the best choice of a husband for Allie."

After what she'd just witnessed, Clarissa was inclined to disagree.

"But being the mature and thoughtful sister that I am—"

"Ha! You hated him until the very moment he begged you to reconsider his suit. And perhaps afterward for a time as well."

For a man whose honor was being maligned, Reid seemed to be taking it all quite well. In fact, he appeared to be enjoying it. Or at least, he enjoyed sitting next to his wife.

All had turned out quite well for them.

Clarissa looked at Aidan again, unable to resist.

He watched the couple as she had been doing. Was he thinking about their situation too? But they were not Allie and Reid. Allie had risked angering her sister. Clarissa risked angering an entire force of well-trained knights under the brutal guidance of a man who hated her. Or at least, thought no more of her than he would his prized warhorse.

Nay, that probably overstated her importance to her father.

"Well, I do not hate him now," Gillian said. "In fact, I believe

I've said this on more than one occasion, but I was wrong. You are, in fact, the most beautiful of couples."

"I've said the same for years," said the deep voice that fluttered Clarissa's insides. "Reid Kerr is the most beautiful man I know." It was the first he'd spoken at the meal.

Everyone at the head table laughed, and none harder than the man at the center of the jest. When Reid looked at his wife, his expression was unmistakable. At least, it was unmistakable to her now. Clarissa knew what it was like to be looked at with desire. With love.

The youngest Kerr stood, pulling Allie up with him.

"Many thanks for a fine meal," he said. "And for your offer to stay for the evening."

He pretended to yawn. "It has been a long journey—"

Again, everyone laughed, knowing it was anything but. Even Father Simon appeared amused.

"And my wife tires easily—"

"Reid!"

Despite her admonition, she stood and took her husband's hand.

"I bid you all a fond farewell for the night," Reid said, taking Allie's hand. With that, the couple descended the stairs of the dais and left the hall amidst the sound of mugs once again pounding on the tables.

Another sound she could never remember hearing at Theffield. And she dared not even consider her time with Lord Stanley, his home even colder and less hospitable than Theffield. Clarissa would prefer to forget she had ever been the wife of such a man.

She wanted this.

Clarissa wanted what Reid and Allie had, and she wanted it with Aidan. From his expression, he was thinking the same.

Clarissa finished her meal in silence, allowing the others around her to guide the conversation. By the time the sweets were cleared, Father Simon had also retired, leaving her with Graeme, Aidan, and Gillian.

"I meant to ask earlier," Gillian said. "Would you like to have your belongings brought into the main keep? There is an empty chamber—"

"Nay," she said, too quickly. Before Aidan could question her motives, she amended, "I am quite comfortable in the Prison Tower for now."

"We really must rename it," Graeme said to Aidan. "It's not been a prison for some years."

Aidan didn't answer. He was watching her, and God help her, Clarissa could not resist him. He looked at her as a man starved, and she understood completely—she felt the same way.

"Shall I escort you to your chamber?"

"Nay," Gillian interrupted. "*I* will escort her. If she will allow it?"

Clarissa looked from Aidan to Gillian, not understanding what was happening. Something was afoot, though perhaps this was for the best. She needed time to think, and if there was one thing she could not do with Aidan afoot, it was thinking clearly.

"Of course, I would be honored," she said, standing. "Graeme, Aidan."

Clarissa caught the look Graeme gave his wife as he bid them good eve. It was a look of promise. A look she was beginning to know well.

"Good eve, ladies," Aidan said, standing. "We shall speak in the morning."

"Aye," Clarissa said. "We shall indeed."

In the meantime, Clarissa had some questions for Gillian.

AIDAN COULDN'T SLEEP.

He'd tried, and failed, finally giving in to the urge to rise despite the early hour. Dressing quickly, he made his way to the great hall. It was still dark outside, the castle mostly still slumbering, with the exception of a few inhabitants whose jobs required an early start. His brother sometimes rose early as well, but Graeme was nowhere to be seen. Aidan walked without knowing where he was going, surprised to find himself in the quiet of Highgate's modest chapel. He used to take mass each morning, though he'd never done so with the vigor of his mother, who'd credited all that happened in the world to the hand of God. Even when she had been too ill to walk to the chapel, she'd insisted on receiving communion each day in her chamber.

The will of God, she'd called her sickness.

He hadn't come back since.

He knelt at the altar, the smell of incense reminding him of their new priest, one whom Aidan did not care for. They'd spoken of replacing the man—his judgmental stare was the most pleasant thing about him—but Graeme was hesitant to do so.

And yet Aidan found himself kneeling here, waiting for the sun to rise.

Waiting to speak to Clarissa.

Waiting for his future to be decided.

He'd dreamt last night that her father had come to Highgate End, demanding to take her back to England. When Aidan awoke, he had, for a brief moment, thought the dream real. The very notion of Clarissa falling into that man's clutches again made him nauseous.

"'Tis early, my son."

He'd heard the noise of footsteps behind him, but he'd assumed it was their priest. On a different day, he would have been relieved to see Father Simon instead.

"Good morn, Father," he said as the priest knelt beside him. "Did you sleep well?"

Mayhap a foolish question considering the early hour, but Father Simon surprised him by nodding.

"Very well indeed."

"But the hour—"

"Is the one I enjoy most," he said, looking around the chapel. "None but myself and God to speak to. It reminds me of my time in the monastery."

"The silence?"

"Aye, and peace that comes from spending the dawn of the day with your own thoughts."

Aidan had always disliked being alone, so to him, such a life seemed more like hell than heaven. But the priest evidently disagreed.

"I would ask what brings you here at this hour, but I believe I already know the answer."

"How much do you know, Father?"

Those knowing eyes met and held his gaze. "Well, son, I know you are in love with a woman who has decided to pledge her life to God."

Aidan blinked.

"Or at least, one who considered doing so before her path crossed with yours."

Of course . . . he knew everything. He always seemed to know everything, even when they and Clan Kerr had been at odds over Lady Catrina. The priest had been the first to suggest a meeting between their clans after she'd married the Englishman rather than Graeme.

"But you came anyway—"

"The nuns agreed to take her."

"You could have sent a message."

"Allie would not allow me to do so."

Allie. The same woman who had urged Aidan to go to Clarissa at Sutworth. Why was she pushing her toward accepting a place at Burness Abbey? It made no sense.

"She urged you to come here? To convince Clarissa—"

"Not to convince, Aidan, but to offer the lady what she asked for, an alternative to the life her father had predestined for her."

Aidan did not want to get angry with the man who tried to help them, in a chapel of all places, but his words were an unwelcome reminder that Clarissa was not yet his. Even as he knew the final choice was, of course, hers alone to make.

But still. "*I* am her alternative," he said.

"Hmmm."

Father looked up at the altar but otherwise said nothing.

"You don't approve?"

His expression unreadable, Father Simon offered only silence. His inscrutable, knowing expression was likely to drive Aidan mad.

"You believe I'm making a mistake. Putting a target on Clan Scott for the sake of a woman?"

Still, silence.

"Graeme supports me in this. Father, she offered herself to the church only because she had no other way to escape her father. But she has another choice now. I love her and cannot lose her."

Again, nothing.

Finally, Father Simon looked at him.

"And what makes you believe you will lose her?"

A chill ran through his body, the words sticking in his throat.

"Aidan?"

He'd have uttered a blasphemy if he wasn't in the company of a priest. Finally, the words came out. "I believe she is still considering your offer."

Father Simon waited.

"She believes the risk is too great. She's agreed to marry me, but . . ."

"But?"

"She feels guilty for all that has transpired. But Father"—he warmed to his argument now—"you do not know Clarissa as I do." Aidan then found himself telling the priest all that he had told Allie, and more.

"She feels badly for telling her father about us," Aidan said, finishing his tale. "He has made her feel inferior, which clearly she is not. And Lord Stanley . . . she needs to understand that the decision is not between staying here and being loved or leaving and keeping us safe."

"Is it not?" Father Simon asked, his expression still unreadable.

"Nay," he said, standing. "Clarissa must decide between living a new life with me, with Clan Scott, and joining the nunnery to escape her father. This is not about Caxton or the border clans. It is about choosing love over fear. Over her father's hate."

He needed to speak to her.

"Indeed," the priest said.

"Thank you for your guidance, Father," Aidan said, leaving the priest to his prayers.

The last thing he noticed was a slight smile on the priest's face. Sometimes, it seemed, saying nothing was more powerful than speaking.

He had to see Clarissa and end this torment.

Now.

CHAPTER 23

*C*larissa shifted on the hard stone bench, staring at the walkway and thick hedging that surrounded it. She'd wandered into the garden unintentionally. After a fitful sleep filled with dreams of Aidan, she'd risen early. She'd considered visiting Lewis again, but Clarissa decided she wanted to be alone, just not in the small chamber that had begun to feel like a prison in truth. Gillian's words of welcome to their clan weighed on her despite their intended effect.

When she'd first come to Highgate Castle, Clarissa had been content to hide away, safe from her father. But now, thanks to Aidan, she wanted more. To be a part of everything Highgate had to offer. To be with him. She simply had to tell Father Simon she could not go with him because she wished to become Aidan's wife.

So why did she hesitate?

"There you are."

Her shoulders fell at the sound. Clarissa had thoroughly enjoyed Allie's company the evening before, but she wanted to be alone. To think. To make sense of the impossible situation she found herself in this morn.

"When you did not answer at my knock, I worried something had happened. May I sit with you?"

When she walked around to the front of the bench, Clarissa nearly tumbled off her seat. Allie wore . . . "What *are* those?"

She hadn't meant to be rude, but she'd never seen anything like it. On a woman, at least. They looked similar to a boy's breeches, and her shirt . . . "You look—"

"Like a peasant boy?" Allie said with a smirk, sitting down beside her. "I've been told as much, but I rather like to think of this as my training outfit."

Training? Ah, yes. Aidan had mentioned he used to train Allie with the longsword. He said she was quite good, in fact. The idea was utterly unimaginable, and when she tried to conjure an image of her father ever agreeing to such a thing, she could not do so.

"I was headed to the training yard but decided to find you instead. In the event . . ."

She didn't finish her thought.

"In the event?"

Allie sighed, her slim shoulders heaving up and down, and blurted, "You are not coming back with us today . . . are you?"

"How did you know?"

"Please do not take offense, but your eyes are incredibly expressive."

She looked down to hide those expressive eyes. "I've not yet spoken to Aidan."

"I saw him on my way here."

"You did?" Her head tipped back up on its own volition.

"Aye, leaving the chapel. Which is most unusual for him. But then, he has been acting most unusual since you've come into his life." She paused. "Again."

So she knew of their history. From the fond and familiar way Aidan spoke of Allie, Clarissa was not surprised.

They sat in silence, the garden becoming brighter and brighter. Though Highgate had no doubt come to life by now, this area was secluded and pleasant, and the only sound was a distant conversation between birds.

"When I first came to Highgate," Allie finally said, "Aidan welcomed me as if I were already family. Much to my father's umbrage, my intended had died by then, taking his coin with him."

Clarissa knew the story. There were many similarities between the late Earl of Covington and Lord Stanley. Both men, advanced in years, had wished to beget a son with a new wife. Both had used the promise of coin, or land, to meet those ends.

"And your mother?" she asked. She'd often wondered how her own mother would have felt about her betrothal.

"Accedes to my father in all things."

"Even a betrothal to the Earl of Covington?"

"Especially that. We needed the coin desperately. Without him, we would have lost Lyndwood."

Aidan had not told her that. Such stakes would certainly weigh heavily on a lord.

Allie held her gaze for a long moment before speaking again. "I admire you," she finally said.

"Admire me? Why?" she asked, embarrassed by her own vanity for asking.

"When Gillian married Graeme and my father offered my hand to Covington as a replacement, it was the very last thing I wished to do, but I agreed. I didn't consider the ways I might avoid it."

"Could you have come here, to live with your sister, instead?"

After all, running away to Scotland had seemed like a good plan to her. Could Allie have done the same, or was her father as tenacious and unwavering as Clarissa's?

Allie looked down at her hands. "I could have. Gillian came to England to fetch me, insisting I do just that."

"But you refused?"

Allie shook her head. "Aye. In a way. I led her to believe I had a plan to escape, but my only plan was to protect Gillian. Had she brought me here, she would have endangered her relationship with Graeme, and who knows how Covington would have retaliated. I could have lived with being the cause of my parents losing Lyndwood, but not with that. Of course," she added, turning toward her, "the whole thing was my father's fault . . ."

But Clarissa wasn't listening.

Whether she realized it or not, Allie had shifted Clarissa's perspective. What she wanted . . . well, that was clear. She wanted to become the wife of a man willing to risk everything for her. But if she got what she wanted, the very place she wished to call home might crumble to the ground. The very people she loved would be imperiled.

Clarissa felt as if she'd run into the stone wall beside her. Her heartbeat quickened as she thought of what she must do.

"Clarissa?" Allie asked, her voice strained. "Do you need—"

She stood. "I need to speak to Aidan."

"Good," Allie said with a grin. "You should speak with him. I've made a mess of it, but I sought you out to tell you Aidan loves you. I think he always has. And we could not be more pleased by his choice."

Clarissa hated to deceive someone who had been nothing but kind to her. But if she told Allie what she planned, she would attempt to talk her out of it.

"When are you leaving?" And then, realizing she may have sounded too hopeful, she added, "I meant to ask, will you be staying for much longer?"

"Nay," Allie said, standing with her. "Reid wants to get back, to await word of Caxton and make plans for the next Day of Truce."

Clarissa squared her shoulders. With any luck, her father would honor his agreement and there would *be* a next Day of Truce.

"I understand," she said.

And I understand what I must do.

AIDAN LOOKED EVERYWHERE for Clarissa before finally going into the hall to break his fast. He hoped she would eventually join them as she'd done the night before, but she did not. He would have left the meal early to search for her had Allie not stayed him.

"Let her be," she had said. "Clarissa will come when she's ready. I know she loves you."

But she never did—and Father Simon was also suspiciously absent from the meal. Despite his thin frame, the priest could eat. He'd just as soon miss mass than a meal, yet there was no sign of him.

Now, as Aidan stood by the keep's front entrance with Allie and Reid, who were preparing to leave, he looked at the woman he loved in horror. She walked toward him with the missing priest.

He knew at once she'd changed her mind.

"I've been looking for you," she said as she approached him.

Aidan tried not to let his annoyance show. "I was in the hall, breaking my fast. With nearly every other person here—"

"I will leave you alone," Father Simon said. "With luck, there are a few scraps from that meal you mentioned . . ." The quickness with which he scurried away confirmed that the worst had indeed happened.

Allie and Reid also wandered away.

"Please," she said, ushering them to a more private space, an alcove under the covered walkway that ran the length of the keep. "Please listen to me."

His whole body tensed. Listen to her? Nay, she could not ask him to do that, not when—

"I love you," she began.

"So much so that you are leaving with Father Simon?"

When she did not disagree, blood pulsed through him and his hands began to shake.

"I love you so much. You do not understand—"

"Aye, Clarissa. I believe I do," he ground out through gritted teeth.

"If I stay here, if I stay with you, my father will come."

"Let him!"

She reached for him, but Aidan pulled his hand away. He couldn't bear to touch her just now.

"You say that, but when he does—and I know he will—how will you feel then? When the very people you've sworn to protect—"

"I've sworn to protect you, Clarissa. And yet you refuse to let me."

"Mayhap I can protect myself."

So this was about her pride? Proving that she did not need him, or anyone, to help her?

"How? By taking a nun's vow and living the rest of your life less than thirty miles from here? From a clan who would accept you, a man who would die to protect you?"

"That," she said, attempting again to reach out as he, once again, pulled away, "is exactly what I am trying to prevent. Don't you understand? How do you think I will feel if something happens to you because of me? If something happens to Gillian or the babe? Aidan—"

"You don't trust me to protect you?"

"Of course I do, but—"

"Nay, you do not. If you did, lass, we would not be having this discussion. We would ask Father Simon to make our union official, then bid him farewell before we go to my bed to finish what we began at the ruins. You would agree to live here, at Highgate End, for the remainder of your days. You would recognize that you belong here."

Aidan felt as if he'd just finished a workout with the men. He could not think, could not get the words out quickly enough. Somehow he had to make her understand.

Rather than answer him, she bowed her head. It allowed him a moment to think, to consider what might convince her to stay. Perhaps she just needed more time—

"Do not do this today," he said. "I will speak to Reid, ask them to delay their departure—"

"Nay, Aidan, that will not matter. I—"

"One day." Frantic for her to agree, he rushed out his next words. "Give me one day. If you still feel this way on the morrow, then go. But please—"

She looked up then, a single tear pooling in the corner of her eye. He reached out, wiped it away, and then cupped her cheek in his hand.

"One day," he repeated, knowing the exact moment when she acquiesced, the resolve in her eyes turning to sorrow. Nodding silently, Aidan pulled her toward him and held her as if it were the last time he'd ever do so. When she wrapped her arms around him, he felt more victorious than after any battle or tournament.

Now, if only he could get her to stay here, in his arms, for good.

CHAPTER 24

*A*idan cursed his brother, again.

He had only one day to convince Clarissa they belonged together. Only a single day, and Graeme decided it was the perfect time to hold a meeting with the elders. One he claimed had been long overdue. The morning was spent trading insults and bickering, and nothing much came of it. After all, they'd already agreed to continue boycotting the Day of Truce if Theffield did not remove Caxton as planned.

He'd promised Clarissa to send word as soon as the meeting concluded, and he did that now. Aidan considered going to her himself, but he had another idea.

He knew how much Clarissa valued her time with Lewis. He wanted her to understand that here, with him, she was free to do as she pleased. If she wanted to bake bread or help Cook in the kitchen, learn how to wield a longsword like Allie . . . no one would deny her.

After ordering Lewis to take a break, he sent word to Clarissa to meet him at the bakehouse. An odd place to make a final stand, to be sure. But he hoped the symbolism of it would help convince Clarissa she need not sacrifice herself for the sake of their clan.

While he waited, Aidan occupied his hands by tidying up the space, imagining Lewis's surprised expression when he returned. He'd thought she would arrive imminently, her chamber was so close, but there was still no sign of her by the time he finished. Aidan began to pace around the table in the center of the room. He went to the door, looked out, and could see no one.

Where was she?

He sat, trying not to think of the last time he'd waited for Clarissa. This was entirely different. Back then, her father had forcibly removed her from the tournament grounds. No one would keep her from him here.

No one but Clarissa herself.

Debating whether he should wait longer or go looking for her himself, Aidan was relieved to see Morgan walking toward him.

Without Clarissa.

Fear, the kind that gripped one's throat and crawled downward, taking up a more permanent residence . . . the kind he felt while staring down an opponent, knowing the next moment could be his last . . . that kind of fear took hold of him as he watched Morgan approach.

She didn't need to say it, because Aidan already knew.

Clarissa was not coming.

WHEN CLARISSA RODE into Highgate Village, the first person she came across was a cobbler. Standing on the threshold of a small cruck house and flinging epithets at another man who had apparently just visited his shop, he was not the sort of person Clarissa wished to approach. But when he stopped cussing long enough for her to pass, greeting her with a surprisingly civil "my lady," she decided to take a chance and ask for his guidance.

On his advice, Clarissa sought out the services of the reeve she now followed. He'd seemed an ideal candidate to help her—reeves were often the most respected of all the servants, chosen as their leader—and he'd eagerly accepted her simple gold ring as payment for an escort to Burness Abbey.

But as they rode on and on and on, she began to doubt him. Surely they would be there already if it truly lay just thirty miles north of Highgate End?

Aidan's meeting must have ended by now, and no doubt he'd ridden off looking for her. Or maybe he'd be angry enough to gladly give her over to the nuns.

"Eh, this way, milady," the reeve, if he truly were one, called back. They'd come to a fork in the well-worn road, one that looked awfully familiar.

"Master Jon," she said, refusing to continue. "Have we not come to this pass before?"

Though she felt certain she'd been at this same juncture before, Clarissa knew her limitations. She could hardly find her way from the northern gates of Theffield to the southern ones. Even if Burness was due north of Highgate Castle, Clarissa would have gotten lost trying to find it herself.

Ignoring the surge of panic that threatened to take hold of her, she rode up to the reeve and gave him a sharp look.

"Uh, nay, my lady. We've not been here before."

The hesitation in his voice told her otherwise.

"Jon," she said in a tone that would not brook an argument, "what is your role, truly, at Highgate?" And before he could answer, she added, "More importantly, do you know where we are going?"

He looked at the two roads ahead, then at her. Digging something from the pouch that hung by his side, he rode toward her and thrust out his hand.

When he opened his fist, her ring lay in his palm.

"Take it," he said, returning her payment. "We will go back—"

"No, we will not." She would not take the ring. She would not go back. If she went back, she'd be forced to confront her turbulent feelings again, and that she could not do. "You will accompany me to—"

"I know not where Burness Abbey be, milady."

She stared straight through him.

"But I had a horse," he continued, "and—"

"And you planned to share the profit from my ring with the cobbler who sent me to you. The one who claimed you were the reeve?"

Guilty.

"I—"

Clarissa didn't care. She was hot, and tired of riding in circles in the heat, but worst of all, she was scared. Even if the nuns accepted her without Father Simon's intercession, she couldn't fathom facing an entire lifetime without Aidan.

Pushing aside the selfish thought, she narrowed her eyes at her directionally challenged guide.

"We will find it. Together."

She was no fool. Though he may not know where to go, Clarissa knew better than to ride to Burness alone. They were likely no longer on Clan Scott land, and the fear Aidan had instilled in her was healthy enough for Clarissa to forgo a ring she'd intended to give the abbess in exchange for even an unreliable escort.

Listening for her "guide" behind her, Clarissa rode ahead and hoped they were at least traveling in the right direction. "Are we traveling north?" she asked as Jon rode up beside her.

"We are, my lady."

In that he appeared quite confident. Trusting his words, Clarissa fell silent, concentrating on the sound of their horses' hooves as they met the dirt and rocks below them. At least, she attempted to do so. Her thoughts stubbornly refused to be distracted by anything other than . . . him.

It struck her that every time someone in Aidan's life had spoken to her of him, their message had been much the same. He loved her. He'd never acted like this with anyone before. He was a good man.

None of them had faulted her for being English. None had railed at her for being the daughter of the Earl of Theffield.

She was the only one who'd questioned her presence in his life.

But it's selfish to love him when it puts so many in danger.

"Do you trust me to keep you safe?" he'd asked. And she'd said she did. Of course she did. But maybe he was right. If she truly trusted him, why didn't she also trust him to decide the best way forward for his clan?

Because he is thinking with his heart.

A heart so big and full of love, one she'd stabbed as surely as if she'd taken his prized dagger and plunged it into him. Clarissa cringed at the image of how his joyful face must have dropped the moment he learned she was gone, for he certainly would know by now.

Oh God, what have I done?

"My lady!"

But the false reeve's warning had come too late. By the time she realized what was happening, an arm had already snaked around her waist.

She struggled as her attacker plucked her off her horse and flung her across his own lap. For a wild moment, she thought perhaps it was . . . nay. When she strained her neck around, she saw the man was most definitely not Aidan. She didn't recognize him.

Smiling, his teeth as crooked as his grin, he pushed her back against his saddle, which cut into her stomach, jolting her with each step. As she tried to struggle, the pain only increased. But she would not stop trying. She might break her neck, but if Clarissa managed to get away from him . . .

Her last thought after her captor slammed his elbow into the back of her head was that she had made a horrible, terrible, life-ending mistake.

CHAPTER 25

"We have to find her."

Aidan stood in the hall with his sisters-in-law, Graeme, and Father Simon. He'd already wasted too much time waiting in the bakehouse for Clarissa to arrive. Perhaps he'd still be there, broken, if Allie hadn't found him.

The dull ache in his chest had turned to raw fear in an instant. He'd assumed she was with Reid and Allie, that his silver-tongued Clarissa had convinced them to take her to Burness Abbey. Upon realizing the awful truth—that she'd gone alone—he'd gathered the others together to arrange a rescue mission. Aye, they needed to find her, but there were multiple roads she could have taken.

"I will take the old Roman road," he announced. "Graeme—"

"North Ridge Way," his brother said. "Let's go."

"We'll send others on less likely paths, to be safe."

"Aidan, wait."

He and Graeme were already heading for the door when Allie stopped him.

"There's no time."

"You should know . . . this may be my fault," Allie blurted.

He waited for her to explain, and when she didn't, he was not feeling generous.

"Allie, what the hell do you mean?"

Her eyes darted to Reid, who'd followed Graeme and Father Simon out of the hall.

"I . . . we talked this morning, in the garden. And . . . oh God, I am so sorry."

"What . . . did . . . you . . . say . . ."

"It wasn't until we realized she was gone that I considered our conversation more carefully. We spoke of Covington and . . ." She swallowed hard. "She asked why I did not flee to Highgate End to escape the marriage."

Aidan didn't have time for this. "Allie—"

"I . . . told her that I stayed behind because I worried what would happen to Gillian if I broke the betrothal."

"You told her the truth."

Allie nodded, tears forming in the corner of her eyes.

He reached her in two strides. Wrapping his arms around her, he hugged his sister-in-law. "I would never fault you for telling the truth, Allie. It is not your fault she left. Clarissa has been scared from the moment we met. And 'tis something none of us can overcome for her."

Releasing her, Aidan left to join the others. They would find her.

She may already be at Burness Abbey. She may already have joined the order.

The thought nearly brought Aidan to his knees. If she was already there, it was by her choice. But if not . . .

God, please do not let any harm come to her.

"Ready?" Graeme asked as he approached them.

He wasn't, not really, but there was no hope for it. Grateful for his brother, who took charge, sending men out in every north-ward direction, Aidan mutely followed the others out of the great gatehouse. When Reid and Graeme took off on their respective paths, Aidan continued on his own—the most likely route to Burness Abbey. He told himself to slow down. Putting himself at risk would not help Clarissa's cause, but his mind kept spinning ever-worsening visions of what could happen to her.

He was so distraught, he very nearly missed it.

Aidan wasn't sure what made him look down at that exact moment, but he reared up at the sight of a glint of gold. Dismounting, he picked up the ring and immediately recognized it as Clarissa's. Every hair on his body stood up straight as he searched the area.

Nothing except for dirt upset with the imprint of hoofmarks.

Something had happened.

Back on his horse, Aidan gripped the reins so tightly his knuckles turned white. He'd vowed to protect her, a vow he'd failed to uphold, but Clarissa was out here somewhere, and he *would* find her. And neither God nor the saints could save anyone who dared harm her.

"AYE, JON. I AM FINE."

She'd repeated the phrase so many times that Clarissa was sure he did not believe her. Perhaps because it was not exactly true. Her head hurt, but as she touched a finger to it, blood no longer stained her fingers. The small wound had dried, and though she knew little about injuries, Clarissa was sure it was not serious.

When she made the perhaps reckless decision to scramble for the dirk at her captor's side, the thought of falling and breaking her neck had been real, but also had the visions of what her captor planned for her. He'd stopped briefly, just once, and allowed her to sit up in front of him. That's when she noticed the dagger. The scene flashed before her again.

His smell nearly gagged her, but more importantly, they were stopped.

It had been the opportunity she'd waited for.

"What in the devil . . ."

Clarissa had stolen the small dagger and jammed it deep into his leg.

"God's blood," he roared as she'd taken advantage of his scream of surprise.

She fell, none too gracefully, from his horse. Her head had cracked the road, but Clarissa could not pause to bemoan the wound. Picking herself up, a quick feel of her temple confirming she had been, in fact, bleeding, Clarissa did the only thing she should.

Ran.

Clarissa knew she could not outrun a horse. There were trees, aye, but none thick enough for her to hide in. And her attacker would likely have been able to find her.

But that's when she spotted Jon.

Clarissa had never seen a sight so welcome as the fletcher. As they rode, every noise making Clarissa jumpier than she was already, she learned the arrow maker had recently come to Highgate looking for work. She also learned that her unlikely helper had lost the gold ring in his hurry to rescue her from the reiver.

A good man, though a terrible guide.

Jon's scream pierced the otherwise tentative quiet, sending her heart leaping into her throat. Luckily, she sat in front of him, so when he toppled to the ground, she managed to stay seated. Had the reiver come back? Was her friend dead? Clarissa dismounted before she could think it through, intent on helping Jon.

An anguished voice stopped her.

"Clarissa."

She had just knelt beside the fletcher. Blood oozed from a dagger wound in his shoulder onto the dirt road beneath him.

"Aidan?"

He pulled her up so quickly, Clarissa would have fallen had he not steadied her.

"He's hurt." She tried to pull away.

Aidan spun her around, his gaze finding the wound on her head. "What happened to you? Did he—"

Finally breaking free, she scrambled back down to the ground. "He's hurt," she repeated. "His shoulder . . . Aidan, do something."

When Aidan didn't move, she realized how he had come by that wound. A dagger handle stuck out of his shoulder. She was going to be ill. Aidan had . . . he must have thought . . .

She stood and shoved him toward Jon, words tumbling out of her. "He did not hurt me. I hired him as a guide. He's from Highgate, the—"

"Fletcher." Finally, Aidan knelt down beside them. "How did he . . . Clarissa, did he do that to you?"

While Jon bled to death, Aidan glared at her head. Nay, nay, she could not allow him to die!

"Nay, it was not him," she shouted. "I will explain later. Will you please help him?"

Jon groaned in response.

With a final glance at her, Aidan said, "Turn your head."

She trusted him, and so she did as he asked.

Aidan was here.

She'd hardly had time to reconcile that fact in all the excitement. Had he come looking for her? She'd wondered if he would be too angry to want her back. Too angry to look for her. But this was, after all, Aidan. Protecting others was his specialty.

"Clarissa, hand me my waterskin."

It took a moment for her to find it. When she turned back around, Clarissa froze.

Aidan was not wearing a surcoat. Or a shirt. His broad muscled shoulders moved in perfect unison as he ripped his linen shirt to shreds.

"Clarissa? The skin?"

"Ah . . . aye . . . the skin." Thrusting it into his hands, she watched as Aidan proceeded to clean and wrap Jon's wound. Or, more precisely, she watched his bare forearms as they worked quickly to bind the fletcher's shoulder.

When she finally realized Jon was watching her watch Aidan, it was too late. Clarissa turned away from his knowing smile.

"Will he . . . live?" she asked Aidan in an undertone.

He laughed. The man actually laughed.

The devil take him.

"Aye, lass, he'll live."

Aidan stood and helped Jon to his feet. "Can you ride?"

Jon nodded. "Aye, milord."

Aidan walked with him back to his mount. "I will escort the lady north," he said. "Go back to Highgate and see that wound properly cleaned."

But though he mounted, Jon did not move to do Aidan's bidding.

"Can you find Highgate?" Aidan asked Jon.

Jon glanced at Clarissa, as if urging her to speak. She cleared her throat, gaining Aidan's attention.

He turned to her, and Clarissa could have wept for the trouble she'd caused. Because of her, poor Jon had been wounded by Aidan's hand. How he'd managed to sink a dirk into the man's shoulder was a question for another time. She had neither seen nor heard him approach—nor had she seen the dagger that had evidently flown past her head.

Clarissa shuddered.

Aidan watched her.

"Jon and I . . ." She cleared her throat again. "We were not riding north," she said, her voice shaking, though not nearly as violently as her hands. It was all simply too much.

"We were returning to Highgate End."

CHAPTER 26

*C*larissa had told him the tale of the reiver who'd attempted to kidnap her, but she hadn't yet told him why she'd headed back to Highgate rather than north to Burness Abbey. Aidan tightened his arm around her, thinking of how close she'd come to real harm. Without the threat of the Day of Truce to curb their behavior, reivers had begun to slowly reclaim the authority they'd lost over the years.

Raids on fellow clans, enemies, or even allies who had broken promises—those had never truly ceased. But the days of reivers kidnapping women or murdering other travelers for a perceived offense had ceased to become a daily part of living along the borders.

"How is your head?" he asked, knowing they were close to Highgate.

"It hurts," she replied, her voice low. "Aidan, we need to talk."

"Aye, we do." He had so many questions, he didn't know where to start. So he remained silent, letting himself soak in the relief that she was okay, as they rode up to the gatehouse. Jon had refused Aidan's offer to be seen by Highgate's physician. He shrugged off the injury, saying he deserved the punishment for attempting to deceive Lady Clarissa.

Allie came running toward them the moment they entered the inner ward, reaching them as they arrived at the stable. "Oh dear. Aidan . . . you've lost your shirt."

Aidan dismounted, whispered something to Allie, and helped Clarissa dismount as well. Then he looked down, feigning surprise.

"I'd not noticed," he said, but Allie was not listening to him. She'd thrown her arms around Clarissa, and the two embraced as if they'd not seen each other in some time. When Allie began to cry, Clarissa looked at him with wide eyes. His chest constricted as he realized that no one had likely ever expressed that type of emotion over her before.

"I am so glad you've returned," Allie said. "We were worried. Graeme came back from the abbey just moments before you arrived. When he said you were not at Burness . . . this was all my fault. Don't shake your head at me, Aidan. It was my fault. I am so, so sorry."

Allie hugged her again, and Aidan waited not so patiently for his sister-in-law to allow Clarissa to breathe.

"Are you here to stay?" Allie asked.

Every muscle in Aidan's body tensed as he awaited her answer. She'd left him, again. Even so . . .

"I . . . I must speak to Aidan," she said.

Disappointment knifed him in the gut. So she'd only returned for a temporary respite from her adventures. Clarissa was still planning to leave.

Aidan turned from the women—

"Wait," Clarissa called out.

But he could not do this now. "See to her head," he called back to Allie.

Aidan didn't know where he was going. He knew only he

could not talk to her. She'd torn his heart from his chest, twice, and he'd be damned if he would let her do it again.

Clarissa followed him.

He spun around. "When you leave next time, please take an escort. Promise me, Clarissa."

"But, Aidan, I—"

This time, he did not stop. Aidan stormed up to the door of the main keep and opened the door himself. He strode through it and kept going. He'd found her, and she was safe.

That was all that mattered. The rest was not his to decide.

"Dammit," he cursed, making his way toward his chamber. He needed a shirt. And a drink. Nay, he needed more than that, but a shirt and an ale would do for now.

The soft sound of footfalls reached his ears.

"Aidan."

He stopped, closed his eyes, and attempted to calm his rapidly beating heart.

"Aidan . . . ," she repeated.

He didn't expect her to touch him, so when she laid a hand on his back, just below his shoulder, he didn't have time to temper his reaction. His heart beat at what was surely a dangerous pace.

"I don't need an escort to Burness Abbey."

His fingers ached with the need to touch her back.

"Did you hear me? Aidan, I'm sorry. I should not have left."

They were the words he'd wanted to hear on their way back to Highgate. The words he had not dared hope for. He simply had to turn around, grab her hand and make her his. Now. This very moment.

So simple.

He stepped forward, away from her, instead.

"Nay, lass," he agreed. "You should not have left."

And then he walked away.

SHE DESERVED THAT.

Clarissa sagged against the stone wall in the hall, her feet unable to move, her body heavy.

She'd hurt him again, as she'd known she would. Terribly. Before, he'd been able to blame her father for taking her away. This time, there was no one to blame but herself.

"Clarissa?"

She stood up once again, embarrassed to have been caught in such a position.

"Gillian." She turned to greet the lady of Highgate.

"Our physician is here. Aidan sent for him to look at your head. Will you come with me to the solar and allow him to examine it?"

Aidan sent for him.

Of course he had. Her chest constricted at the memory of him standing in front of her, his back to her.

And oh my . . . what a back it was. When she'd touched him—

"This way," Gillian said.

Clarissa's cheeks flooded with heat. She'd made the worst decision of her life, and still she stood here thinking of Aidan in that way. A lump formed in her throat. No, no . . . she would not cry. Not in front of Lady Gillian.

"So tell me, what happened to your . . . oh, Clarissa . . ."

She could no sooner stop the tears from falling than she could take back the miserable excursion that had earned her Aidan's disdain.

"Come here," Gillian said, holding Clarissa as if she were a newborn babe. It was too late to stop the tears now. Her shoulders shook with the pain of her decisions.

"I only wanted to protect him," she muttered against Gillian's shoulder.

"I know you did. He knows that too."

"No, I've ruined everything. He hates me—"

Gillian pushed her away gently and frowned.

"Nay, he does nothing of the sort. Aidan loves you, Clarissa. Everyone can see that. He may be angry, but that doesn't change the way he feels about you."

Gillian reached up and wiped her cheek with the back of her hand. How could this woman, a stranger, be kinder to her than her own father? How could she care for her more than the man who'd brought her into this world?

Holding her gaze, Gillian added, "And I know you love him too." She crossed her arms over her chest. "So, the question remains, what will you do about it?"

And she'd thought the woman so sweet.

"I suppose I should find him, tell him—"

But Gillian was already shaking her head. "Those are just words. You need to show him."

"Show him?"

Clarissa was prepared to do anything it took. She'd realized something after her near miss with the reiver. She valued herself —and her happiness. And she was willing to fight for it. Despite the harsh words her father and former husband had spewed, she *was* worthy.

"Aye." She wiped away the last vestiges of the tears that would not help her win Aidan back. "I will show him," she promised, "and when I win him back, I will never, ever leave again."

———

"You look beautiful. Doesn't she look beautiful?" Allie asked her sister.

Clarissa could not believe how perfectly Gillian's gown fit her. When she'd tried to go back to her chamber in the Prison Tower after the physician's examination, Gillian had refused to allow it. In fact, Clarissa's belongings, which she'd left behind, were already being brought into the main keep.

On Gillian's orders, a tub had been brought to the lord and

lady's chamber for Clarissa, and when Graeme had attempted to come into the room earlier to prepare for the evening meal, his wife had told him to leave. Clarissa had argued against it. After all, winning back Aidan's heart should not involve angering his brother and the chief of his clan. But Gillian had not accepted no for an answer.

Fiona and Morgan had flitted in and out of the room, helping Clarissa prepare for supper, and by the time they were finished with her, she had to admit she'd never felt so fussed over in her life. The navy blue gown Gillian had foisted on her suited her perfectly, ornamented simply with a silver belt, and her hair had been brushed until it was gleaming as brightly as a newly polished piece of armor. Clarissa had tried to pull it back, away from her face as was her custom, but the women insisted she leave it down.

"I will not take that gown back," Gillian said, looking at her with an assessing eye. "It was made for you."

"No, no, I cannot—"

"Clarissa." Gillian took her hands, a wonder she could find them amidst the folds of fabric. "You are our sister now—"

"Nay, I am not—"

"Aidan will not stay angry with you." Gillian looked at Allie. "Will he stay angry?"

"I should think not," Allie said, grinning.

"You are a member of Clan Scott, and we will love and protect you, always. The gown?" She dropped her hands and stood back to look Clarissa up and down again. "'Tis a gift, so you cannot give it back."

The words elicited yet another wave of emotion.

Oh no, not again . . .

"No," Allie yelled. "You cannot cry!"

She had to laugh at the panicked look on her face, and that laughter chased away the tears. For the first time, she felt part of a family, a true family. If only she could keep them. Though Gillian and Allie seemed quite confident, Clarissa was not so sure she would be forgiven.

"We've told Graeme and Reid to meet us in the hall. So whenever you're ready," Allie said, grabbing her hand.

"And if I'm not ready yet?"

Allie pulled her, laughing. "'Tis no matter. You're coming anyway."

She followed the women through darkened corridors lit only by wall torches. For its many similarities to Theffield Castle, Highgate seemed to glow just a bit brighter everywhere they went. There was more activity, the sounds of the great hall already reaching their ears as they made their approach. And certainly there were more smiles, including the ones on her friends' faces. They both beamed with delight as they ushered Clarissa into the hall. Neither seemed to be bothered by the sudden hush that descended around them.

"Keep walking," Gillian whispered. She hadn't realized she'd stopped at the entrance, looking for him. Clarissa should wonder at the sudden quiet. She should worry it was due to her, the woman that had led half of Theffield on a merry chase earlier in the day. Clarissa should wonder what everyone knew of her, exactly.

But she did not care at this very moment. Maybe she would later, but right now she only cared about seeing Aidan. And then she did.

Unfortunately, he now donned both a shirt and a surcoat.

Had Allie and Gillian dressed her in dark blue apurpose, knowing he would be wearing the same color?

Though he had not shaved, the stubble across his jaw made him appear fiercer than usual. Or perhaps she only thought so because she'd witnessed him toss a dagger into poor Jon from atop his horse.

As she walked toward the raised dais, she could see the slight curls in his hair that told her it had been recently wet. A bath? The river?

Clarissa forced herself to look away.

When she was guided to the seat next to him, she was none too surprised. She glanced at Allie and Gillian, whose secret smiles told her they had planned the seating arrangements as well.

The thought loosened her limbs, made her feel as if she were walking on air instead of a hard, rush-laden ground. Clarissa took a step up and was greeted by a standing Aidan, whose hand guided her to the seat next to him.

"Thank you," she said, sitting, the velvet cushion under her soft and inviting.

"In England, the lord's brother would be seated next to him," she said. Instead, she and Aidan sat at the very end of the dais.

"The same is true here."

Aye, Gillian and Allie.

"You are in high spirits," Aidan said, his voice strained.

As their goblets were filled with wine, Clarissa tried to calm herself, but the air between them smelled of Aidan. Warmth radiated from him. Calm? Nay, it would not happen. "I am glad to be here."

She would not hide anything from him this eve.

Aidan said nothing.

She had decided Aidan de Sowlis would be her husband, but she hadn't thought it would be easy to persuade him she'd changed her mind. Well, she was nothing if not patient. She stayed as silent as he, waiting for an opportunity.

Her wait was rewarded when their meal was placed before them. Just as he reached for a slice of cheese from their shared trencher, she did the same. Her fingers not so accidentally touched his, though she pulled back, as if startled.

Clarissa was rewarded with a sharp glance.

Did he know she did it apurpose?

Though neither of them spoke, her next opportunity came as

they finished the first course. When Aidan handed her the cleaning cloth, she ensured their fingers touched once again. This time, she allowed hers to linger.

A tick in his jaw told her it was working.

Throughout the meal, he spoke mostly to Allie, who sat on his left. Conversation with her was limited to pleasantries, but Clarissa was not fooled by his casual manner. Twice she'd caught him looking at her as if she were an interesting specimen who required further study.

At one point, a servant placed a jug of wine in front of Aidan, assuring them he would soon return, to see to another task. Rather than wait, Clarissa murmured, "Pardon me," and reached across the trencher for the jug. And if her leg brushed his under the table, well, it couldn't be helped.

The hand on her knee so startled her, Clarissa nearly dropped the wine.

"What are you about, my lady?"

His hand remained in place, the heat of it searing into her.

"I am attempting to pour more wine," she said, refusing to look away. His eyes, anything but cool, bore into her own.

"Nay, you are attempting to seduce me," he said in a lowered voice.

She pretended to be shocked by his directness.

"I promise you, Aidan, I've not seduced any man before in my life."

Though he relaxed his grip, Aidan's hand still did not move.

"But you don't deny you are doing just that now?"

Can I be so bold as to admit it?

Had she not just stabbed a man in the thigh?

"Nay, I do not deny it."

His thumb moved ever so slightly, caressing her. And then it was gone.

"Why?" He took the jug and poured her wine without looking away.

"I'm sorry," she said, lowering her voice. "I should not have left."

He didn't respond, but neither did he look away.

"I will never leave you again."

She desperately needed him to believe her, but Clarissa could tell he did not. Yet. At least he was listening.

"I would do *anything*," she said, putting emphasis on that last word, "to prove it to you."

Finally, a crack. His lips parted, ever so slightly. She did not relent.

Leaning closer to ensure they could not be heard, she whispered, "I am yours. Let me show you that I will always be so."

He turned to her so abruptly that their lips almost touched. Leaning back, Clarissa gripped the stem of her goblet more tightly.

"Anything?"

"Anything," she said, her voice firm and her resolve even more so.

The corner of his lips rose, ever so slightly, and Clarissa nearly melted into her seat. It was the first time he'd smiled all day.

He took a swig from his drink, not bothering to look if anyone else had noticed them. Which they hadn't. Or at least they'd pretended not to.

Aidan was watching her now, a probing stare that sent shivers down her spine and to her very core.

"In that case—" he placed the goblet back onto the table and leaned toward her, "—I would wed and bed you, my lady." Before she had time to be surprised by his bluntness, he added, "Though not necessarily in that order."

CHAPTER 27

"Father, may I speak with you?"

The meal had ended some time ago. Clarissa had left the hall with Allie and Gillian, their knowing so unmistakable, he'd almost laughed at them. His sisters had clearly decided to involve themselves in his romance, and he could not say he minded. He'd stayed to speak with Graeme and Reid, who had been even more direct in their encouragement. They, too, had retired for the evening, but Aidan had elected to wait for Father Simon, who'd gone to the village. The priest had arrived a few moments before, but Aidan had waited for his food to arrive before asking anything of him.

"Of course, Aidan. How may I be of assistance?"

The priest sat in front of a trencher of food piled high by servants who clearly knew the man well.

"You will forgive me if I eat?" Father asked. "I did not expect to be gone so long."

"Of course." He waved his hand, indicating that he should do so. "You have heard Clarissa has returned?"

Father Simon nodded, though a mouthful of bread and cheese prevented him from speaking.

"I would like you to marry us tomorrow, before you leave."

Father stopped chewing. When he resumed, Aidan held his breath.

"Can I assume the lady is in agreement?"

Aidan thought of her reaction when he'd so crudely asked her that very question. As always, her thoughts had flitted across her face for the world to see—surprise, then relief, then something more.

From the very moment they'd sat down for the meal, he'd noticed something had changed in her. She was . . . more assured. Full of resolve. And while his anger had taken longer to abate, he'd known all along it wouldn't linger. All he had ever wanted was for Clarissa to love herself as much as he loved her. To understand that she was as valuable as any member of their clan. If it took fleeing to Burness and a near-death experience to make that happen . . . then he could almost be thankful events had unfolded in such a way.

Surely Jon would disagree.

"Aye, Father. She is."

Father Simon took another bite, chewing much too slowly for Aidan.

"She'd not have made a very good nun," he said finally.

Laughing, Aidan had to agree. "But she will make the perfect wife. Father, say you will—"

"Of course, I will be honored."

He was about to thank him when Father Simon added, "On the condition that you open yourself to the same God that brought you and Clarissa together."

Aidan's eyes narrowed. "You would bargain with me to take mass?"

"Aye, I would," Father said, clearly unapologetic. With a swig of wine, he added, "So do we prepare for a wedding on the morrow?"

He'd been avoiding mass since his mother had passed, but no

longer. He would look forward, and not back. Tomorrow he would begin his life anew.

"We do." Aidan stood. "Thank you, Father, but I must go—"

He froze when Father Simon cleared his throat. "Son, you understand the proper order of things when it comes to holy matrimony?"

He supposed he could take the priest's advice, leave Clarissa untouched until she became his wife in the morn. After all, he'd waited this long. Could he not wait one more night?

Nay, he could not.

"I do, Father," he said instead. "And will take it under advisement."

He should have said, "I have already taken it under advisement." As he walked out of the hall, he felt sure he heard Father Simon mutter, "No better than a Kerr."

He would take that as a compliment.

Taking the stairs two at a time, Aidan realized that although he'd arranged to meet Clarissa in her new chamber after the rest of the family had retired, he'd failed to ask which room she'd been moved to. He only knew her belongings had been brought from the tower to the keep. No matter. He would find her.

Except the chamber he'd suspected she would be in was empty. Indeed, each door he shoved open on the keep's second floor, the one reserved for guests, was empty. By now Gillian would be abed. He could seek her out, but Graeme would likely not appreciate it. Should he wake Morgan instead? Perhaps the maid was not yet abed.

He took two steps back toward the hall and stopped.

Something Allie had said to him surfaced in his mind. He'd told her about seeing Clarissa again, and how it had made him feel, and she'd responded, "I understand well. It is you who does not understand. But you will."

She'd recognized the depth of his feelings for Clarissa from the start. She'd recognized Clarissa was to be family. He smiled, certain he had solved the riddle.

He went back toward the great hall, this time turning up another corridor and ascending a different set of circular stairs. There were just two chambers up here. One, a smaller version of the solar chamber enjoyed by the lord and lady of Highgate. The other, a much larger room that he and Graeme had once shared as children. It had since been transformed to an adult's bedchamber, the two small beds replaced with a large one, and all vestiges of the lads' childhood removed.

Aidan paused as his hand fell on the iron handle of his bedchamber.

Clarissa would be in there, waiting for him. Waiting for this night and for the beginning of their lives together.

He pushed the door open.

———

THOUGH SHE'D BEEN WAITING for him to arrive, Clarissa startled when the door opened. She'd not been nervous before now, but watching Aidan as he closed the door behind him . . .

"Gillian?" he asked.

Clarissa looked down at her fine cream chemise and then back up to meet Aidan's watchful gaze.

"Allie. The gown was Gillian's."

"Ahhh." He took a step toward her. "They've taken to you, lass."

Clarissa nodded, not trusting her voice.

"And I them."

In three long strides, he reached her, pulling her toward him, and crushed his lips to hers. Clarissa wrapped her arms around him and responded with a tentative touch of her tongue, vowing never to let go. Aidan plunged deeper, his tongue tousling with hers, his head tilting for better access.

This was unlike any of their previous kisses. This one was

meant to claim, and its outcome would ensure it. She had thought perhaps they would talk first. After all, there was much to discuss. But Aidan appeared to have other plans.

When his hand reached for the hem of her chemise, his fingers brushing her flesh, something inside her snapped. She wanted no barriers between them, now or ever.

"Take it off," she said, pulling her lips away for the briefest of moments. Aidan took the opportunity to lift the chemise, and in one fluid motion, he tossed it onto the ground.

But then he stopped.

"I plan to worship every bit of your luscious body before the night is through," he said, staring into her eyes as he spoke.

With that, he lifted her into his arms and claimed her mouth once again. Clarissa, so intent on the feel of the arms cradling her and the firm pressure of his lips, barely registered they were moving before the cool cloth hit her back. She now lay on his bed. Assuming he would join her, Clarissa began to push herself upward, toward the pillows, but Aidan grabbed her ankles to stop her.

"Nay."

Running his hands from her ankles upward, he reached behind her waist and pulled her toward the edge of the bed so her feet now dangled over it. He stood then, pulling his own shirt over his head and tearing off his leather boots as if they offended him.

She attempted to prop herself onto her elbows, but Aidan stopped her.

"Stay where you are," he commanded. "I begin to fulfill my promise now."

"What promi—"

The sight of him kneeling at the foot of the bed confused her. What was he about?

"Relax, my love," he said, gently pulling her knees wide. And then, with the wickedest of grins, he added, "My promise to worship you."

Nothing . . . nothing could have possibly prepared her for the feel of Aidan's tongue on her. She did pull back then, surprised. But his hands reassured her, his thumbs rubbing gently on her inner thighs. When he touched his tongue again, she was prepared.

And worship her he did.

Clarissa grasped the coverlet at her sides as he used his tongue, his lips and, oh God, his fingers to render her incapable of coherent thought. Her legs quivered as she brought her hips up to meet him, and the slight throbbing she'd felt turned into violent pulsing that started at her core and traveled straight up to every other part of her body.

Calling his name over and over again, Clarissa finally opened her eyes and relaxed her grip on the coverlet. He stood between her legs, smiling.

"If you'd done that before, I might not have left."

The sound of his laughter as he walked to the side of the bed sent a different kind of warmth flooding through her. Making upward to join him, Clarissa tried to grab the top of the coverlet to pull it down, but Aidan stopped her.

"Nay," he said. "I would see you as we make love."

And that was when she realized they had only just gotten started.

HE DIDN'T KNOW where to begin.

As he stared down at the perfection of the woman who would be his wife, Aidan worried, for the first time in years, about his ability to prolong her pleasure. He'd thought of this so many times. Dreamed of this very sight, a naked Clarissa in his bed.

When she'd come down to the hall earlier, Aidan had felt sure he'd never see a lovelier sight.

He'd been wrong.

Aidan took a deep breath as he removed his braies and trewes.

"Oh . . . dear." Clarissa's mouth hung open, making it difficult for him to remain humble under her appreciative gaze. Her eyes revealed all, as usual.

"Are you scared?"

"Nay," she said. "But I am surprised."

He wasn't sure he wanted to know why. Instead of responding, Aidan surprised her again by shifting back down to the bottom of the bed. Positioning himself between her legs, he started with her calf, moving quickly to the sensitive flesh behind her knees. As he ran his hands upward, following each touch with a kiss, his lips pressed harder and harder each time. When he reached her hip, he flicked out his tongue. On her stomach, a bit more. By the time he arrived at her breasts, Clarissa reached down and grabbed the hair at the back of his head.

But he didn't need prompting to take the hard peak into his mouth. Or to give her other breast the attention it deserved as well. When his fingers found her, Clarissa was wet, waiting. But it was not time.

Not yet.

First, he wished to hear his name on her lips. He would feel her pleasure beneath his mouth. He would know she had been well pleasured this night, the one just before he made her his in truth. When she closed her fists in his hair, he did not let up. Just the opposite in fact. He caught her cries with a searing kiss, thoughts of hearing his name forgotten in a rush of pleasure so powerful Aidan knew he'd not last much longer.

Without giving her time to recover, Aidan pulled away and watched the haze of her climax begin to lift.

"Marry me. Tomorrow."

Her lips, slightly parted and glistening from his kiss, were too tempting. He gave in, just one small touch of his lips.

"But how—"

"Father Simon has agreed to say the vows. But if you would rather wait—"

"Nay."

His heart skipped a beat.

"That is to say, nay I do not wish to wait. Tomorrow is a fine day for a wedding."

The look in her eyes told him she was no longer afraid. He'd never felt happier than he did at this moment.

"If we are to marry tomorrow," she asked, "does that mean we will wait until tomorrow night to—"

He'd pushed her legs apart with his knees. But just in case that wasn't enough of an answer, he guided himself to her, entering just enough to give her the answer she sought.

"It will hurt, but not for long. Or so I am told."

Just a bit deeper . . . "How is that?"

Clarissa gripped his shoulders. "It is . . . different than your fingers."

He laughed, both at her words and at her bemused expression.

"I should hope so, lass."

He'd reached the barrier, and she must have felt it too. Leaning down, Aidan used his tongue to coax her lips apart. When they did, he gave her no quarter. Waves of heat shot up from where they were joined, the kiss slowly spiraling out of control.

Good.

When he felt her tighten around him, Aidan thrust into her.

"Tell me when you want me to move again," he said through gritted teeth, fighting the need to thrust again. Arms shaking as he held himself above her, he reminded himself not to look down. Instead, he concentrated on her face, waiting for her to relax.

"I . . . I think you can move."

When he did, it wasn't nearly enough. But she would set the pace, not he.

"Maybe a bit more."

He gave her more, would give her everything if she so desired. Need coiled in his groin, the desire to push so strong—

"Like this." The lass grasped his hips and guided him. He'd have laughed again if he could breathe.

She was going to kill him. Aidan would die the night before his own wedding.

Another push of her hips, and he'd had enough. It was clear Clarissa was ready, and so he gave her what she'd so gently asked for. Aidan gave her all of him. Instead of releasing his hips, she continued to hold on, to push them together. By now he was slamming into her harder than he would have wanted for their first time, but Clarissa showed no signs of relenting. It was only when he began to circle his hips that she let go in favor of gripping the coverlet.

"Aidan, I need—"

"I know what you need, my love."

He kissed her. For every missed opportunity. Every time he'd left her. He kissed her for not having come back for her sooner, for the love that had first budded in his heart the first day they met.

Aidan kissed her for loving him back.

And when she began to pulse beneath him, he kissed her for the powerful throbs that ensured she was his, forever. As she clenched around him, Aidan shattered with her, their cries one. The world ceased to exist. Everything that mattered was here in the aftermath of the most incredible experience of his life.

Like nothing before it.

She was like no one else.

He refused to be separated from her just yet, so he pulled her close and rolled on top of her, wrapping his arms around her. He hadn't held her for long enough when she lifted her head.

"Can we do that again?"

Luckily, his chamber was in an isolated part of the keep, for otherwise his roar of laughter would easily have been overheard.

Before pulling away, he kissed her nose and then nipped at her lower lip.

"As many times as you'd like, lass."

"You knew it would be like that?"

"Well, not precisely—"

"And yet you held yourself back from me?" She shrugged. "I'm not sure I could have done the same."

Saucy lass.

"Says the woman who was less than a sennight away from becoming a nun."

Her eyes widened. At least now she understood.

"How could you have let me even consider such a thing?" she asked, genuinely surprised.

He'd wondered the same.

"That," he tried to explain, "was magnificent. I tried to persuade you of how good we would be together, but I could not decide for you. I'd have been no better than your father had I attempted to do so."

He could tell she understood what he meant.

"Then I'm glad I decided to come back." She looked down at him then, and Aidan felt himself already growing hard.

"As am I."

He could tell the moment she knew, and approved. But when Clarissa attempted to move off of him, he stopped her.

"Nay, lass, stay right there."

"On top of you?"

He groaned. "Aye, on top of me."

"But . . . can I . . . can we—"

"Oh yes, we can."

And he would enjoy showing her how.

CHAPTER 28

$\mathcal{T}$hree days of pure joy.

From *that* *night* to the impromptu but perfect wedding and then their first full day of marriage, the last three days had been the happiest of Clarissa's life. And yet a single shadow hung over them. They still had not received word about who would replace Lord Caxton. Whenever he sensed she was worrying about her father—that he might discover her whereabouts before doing what he'd pledged—Aidan reassured her that all would be well.

She'd begun to believe him.

So when two men she didn't recognize strode into the hall just as they finished the midday meal, the hairs on her arms stood up straight. Aidan's and Graeme's expressions did not help alleviate her worry.

"Who are they?"

"Lawrence's men. Though I don't see him, which is unusual."

"Greetings," Aidan called as he and Graeme stood. "Where is Lawrence?"

The men exchanged glances. Oh God, no . . .

"Is he—"

"Lawrence is well," one of them said. "May we have a word?"

Clarissa stood to leave, the meal having already concluded. Gillian had not been feeling well, so she would go up to see her.

Aidan reached out and took her hand. "Stay."

"But you have matters to attend to—"

"*We* have matters to attend to."

He squeezed her hand before releasing it. Pleased that he wished her to stay, she sat back down. A flurry of activity unfolded in front of her as Graeme cleared the hall, those who'd remained after the meal leaving to attend to their various duties.

"What happened?" Graeme asked as he returned to the high table.

The shorter of the two men spoke.

"A raid," he said, his eyes darting between Graeme and Aidan. "Alec and Lawrence led a hot trod across the border after the perpetrators—"

Alec? Clarissa tried to remember who that might be. Ah, Lawrence's older brother. She'd met him during her stay at their keep.

"One of the thieves was killed by one of our men—"

"Alec ordered everyone back home to Bowden Castle," the taller man said. They were both talking at once now. "But they were attacked by the same family on their return—"

"Alec is dead."

Clarissa gasped.

Aidan's flexed jaw and raised shoulder were the only indication he'd heard that proclamation. Graeme, on the other hand, pounded his fist on the table. "He will be avenged—"

"There's more."

When the two men looked at her, Clarissa's blood ran cold. More? Did it have to do with—

"The reivers claim Caxton is still in power. They bragged of not having to account for their crimes."

"Still in power?"

Aidan, though he would appear calm to one who did not know him well, was seething now in anger.

"Our chief sent us here to deliver a message. Caxton is still warden and will remain as such. The Earl of Theffield had no intention of ever removing him. While he placated Douglas, he was gathering enough men to turn Theffield Castle into an impenetrable stronghold."

"What?" she cried out, unable to stop herself. "He never intended . . ."

She clamped a hand over her mouth. But Aidan nodded his encouragement. "Go on, lass."

Bastard.

Even though she'd initially expected some sort of duplicity, her father's cruelty still surprised her. "I'd begun to believe, though it seemed unlikely, my father was on your side. Or at least, on the side of peace. But if he's been so bold, it can only mean he has the support of the king. They are preparing for war."

No one spoke.

"Lawrence," she asked finally, "where is he?"

She was fond of Aidan's friend and worried for him. "He is with the chief," one of the men replied. "They are burying their own. But they wanted you to know . . . to prepare. We have others to inform—"

"Of course," Aidan said. "Give Lawrence my deepest sympathies—"

Graeme nodded. "And tell the chief of Clan Karyn they have our full support."

They did not smile, exactly, but Clarissa could tell the men were pleased with Graeme's words. When they turned to leave, Graeme excused himself. He would find a servant to give them food to take.

Gillian would be proud. She was always worrying if everyone around them had enough to eat.

"I am so sorry," Clarissa said, turning to face Aidan.

"He was a good man. Lawrence must be devastated."

She hated to think of what it would do to Aidan if something were to happen to Graeme.

"He will never recover." He looked at her expectantly. "But you know what this means? Your father."

"He did not need our marriage as motivation to act against us. He was already doing so."

"It appears war is unavoidable now." Aidan reached for her, and Clarissa gave him her hand. "You being here, with us, is not the cause."

Once, she would have been glad for that. But the thought of Aidan going to battle . . . she shuddered.

"What will happen now?"

He thought for a moment and then stood abruptly, grabbing her hand and pulling her with him.

"Now? We walk."

Hand in hand, she and Aidan left the hall, walked through the courtyard and toward the gatehouse.

"I don't understand," she said. "Why don't my father and Caxton and the others reach out and grab the peace that is right before them? Why allow the border to revert back to the way it was before the truce? This strife does not seem to benefit anyone."

"It benefits those who line their pockets collecting black mal, the bribe money making lords of common men. It benefits those who take advantage of the king's poor health to improve their own status—"

"And my father cares only for garnering favor with such men."

They continued to walk, moving through the gates and down the hill. When she heard no sounds of clanging metal, Clarissa assumed the men trained within the walls today.

"What will happen now?" she asked.

They arrived at the very same river Clarissa had bathed in seemingly so long ago. Now she was a married woman, one who somehow felt protected despite the chaos that erupted around them.

"The clans will officially renounce the Day of Truce. Reivers will continue to take advantage, and this—" he swept his arms up toward Highgate End, "—will become our refuge. Travel may no longer be safe," he added, the regret in his voice surprising.

"You sound sad about that," she said.

Aidan pulled her into his arms and held her close. "You have been sheltered for too long. I had hoped to take you on grand adventures . . ."

She pulled back just enough to look into his eyes. Clarissa wanted to be sure he understood her. "Aidan, being with you has been the grandest adventure of all. I would happily accept being locked away in Prison Tower forever if you were by my side. I love you."

"You gave me your favor once . . ."

"And I would do so again."

He kissed the tip of her nose. "You already have, and I shall treasure the gift of your love, today and always."

EPILOGUE

"*L*ewis, your wife is in the courtyard asking for you."

Which was partly true. The alewife was indeed directing the unloading of her precious cargo. However, she had been on her way to the bakehouse when Aidan had stopped her. He'd offered to send Lewis her way, suggesting her husband could use a break.

"Go," he said, "I can help Clarissa in here."

Lewis looked at him skeptically.

"Your wife," he reminded Lewis, who winked at Clarissa. If they shared a private secret, certainly they'd not let him in on it. Her bond with the baker was one of many she'd developed with the people of Clan Scott, though Aidan was not surprised.

"And what do you know of baking bread?" Clarissa asked when he joined her. He waited a moment longer, until Lewis had indeed left, then pulled his wife's hands from the dough she'd been shaping.

"Less than I know about pleasing my wife," he said, leaning toward her. The smell of freshly baked bread mixed with the scent of Clarissa's hair was a heady combination that made him wish Lewis would not be returning.

When his lips touched hers, the already hot room grew even warmer. Or perhaps he just imagined it to be so. Either way, it did not take long for the quick kiss to turn into something much, much deeper.

Grabbing her none too gently, Aidan pressed Clarissa to him.

"Aidan, we cannot—"

She gasped as he showed her how quickly he'd become aroused. Celebrating his victory, Aidan tilted his head to deepen the previously chaste kiss. This one was anything but.

Hot, demanding . . . it promised to put a mutually pleasurable end to what he'd started. Her breasts both soft and firm against him, Aidan tried hard not to imagine what they'd looked like that morn, unbound and beautiful, but he failed miserably. Groaning, he began to move toward the door.

"What are you . . . how is this helping Lewis?"

Aidan had forgotten all about the baker and his bread.

"I do not believe it will. But"—he moved toward the door—"it will help me very much."

With a roll of her eyes, Clarissa said, "I do not doubt it, but there are many loaves yet to—"

He silenced her with another kiss.

Perhaps Aidan should feel poorly for not allowing her to finish. But he did not. The men's training had concluded for the day, as had his meeting with Graeme and the elders. Nothing prevented him from scooping her up and carrying her to their bedchamber . . . nay, they would go to her former room in the tower. It was much closer.

Nothing, that is, save for his wife.

"If you wish to stay," he cupped her bottom in both hands, "then you shall, of course, stay."

Circling his hips, he watched her expressive eyes, waiting for . . . *that*.

And then, he struck. "But if you will allow me instead to take you just over there—" he nodded toward the tower, "—I can assure you it will be worth it."

He didn't break eye contact.

He didn't move his hands except to give her bottom a slight caress.

She sighed, and Aidan knew he'd won.

But just as he was about to rejoice in his victory, the door opened and he let go of Clarissa instinctively.

Lewis looked back and forth between the two of them.

"I apologize," Aidan said, "for stealing your most loyal servant. I promise to return Clarissa shortly."

His poor wife's cheeks had turned pink, but he wasn't sorry. Grabbing her hand, he took two steps toward the door before Lewis's voice stopped him.

"When you return her," he said. "You may want to visit the laundress next."

He followed Lewis's gaze to his black tunic, now covered in bread dough. His laughter followed them out into the sunlight.

"I SHOULD GO."

Though she was the one who'd said the words, Clarissa didn't move. As much as she loved working alongside Lewis, being tucked in the arms of her husband was even more enjoyable.

"Aye, lass, you should."

She allowed her fingers a bit of exploring, watching as little bumps formed on his chest wherever she trailed her touch.

"I forgot to ask about the meeting."

His hand stopped hers as it moved lower.

"If you truly do wish to assist Lewis this afternoon, then you ought to stop there."

Chuckling, she wound her fingers into his.

"It went . . . as expected."

Though the past weeks had been kind to them, nearly every day some reminder of the events that had taken place just beyond their land gave her pause.

"Another great council has been called, but this time at Brockburg."

"So close to the border?"

"Aye, it will be a meeting of borderers from both sides."

That surprised her. "From England?"

"Aye, and the border clans here. A meeting of all those loyal to peace."

"What outcome do they hope for?"

When Aidan didn't answer, she looked up.

"A good question, my love. Without any support from your English king?" He shrugged.

"And you are attending?" She tried to keep the worry from her voice.

"I am, in Graeme's stead. It should be interesting, indeed. 'Tis rumored young Neill Waryn has returned from the south with news that will impact all involved."

"Reid's brother-in-law?"

"Aye, love."

"What news does he bring?"

When Aidan released her fingers, she knew he was finished speaking of border politics. And when his hand not so subtly reached for her breast, Clarissa had a feeling her duties with Lewis were indeed done for the day.

The turmoil outside Highgate Castle walls grew, but so did her passion. So, placing all thoughts of battle plans aside, she seized the moment. Putting Aidan's very detailed instructions from the evening before to good use, she heeded his advice. *Enjoy the love and protection our clan will always provide. And if you are troubled, allow me to distract you.*

ENJOY THIS BOOK?

Reviews are extremely important for any author and an essential way to spread the word about the Border Series. There is nothing more important that having a committed and loyal group of readers share their opinion with the world.

If you enjoyed this book, I would be extremely grateful if you could leave a short review on the book's Amazon page. You can jump there now by clicking the link below. Thank you in advance.

Review The Rogue's Redemption

BECOME AN INSIDER

The best part of writing is building a relationship with readers. Become a CM Insider to receive a FREE copy of *The Ward's Bride: Border Series Prequel Novella* and a bonus chapter of *The Thief's Countess*. The CM Insider is also filled with new release information including exclusive cover reveals and giveaways with links to live videos and private Facebook groups so I can get to know my readers a bit more.

CeceliaMecca.com/Insider

ALSO BY CECELIA MECCA

The Border Series

The Ward's Bride: Prequel Novella

The Thief's Countess: Book 1

The Lord's Captive: Book 2

The Chief's Maiden: Book 3

The Scot's Secret: Book 4

The Earl's Entanglement: Book 5

The Warrior's Queen: Book 6

The Protector's Promise: Book 7

The Rogue's Redemption: Book 8

The Guardian's Favor: Book 9 (Dec. 2018)

Enchanted Falls

Falling for the Knight: A Time Travel Romance

Bloodwite

Also love PNR? Vampires are coming in January 2019!

ABOUT THE AUTHOR

Cecelia Mecca is the author of historical and paranormal romance, including the bestselling Border Series, and sometimes wishes she could be transported back in time to the days of knights and castles. Although the former English teacher's actual home is in Northeast Pennsylvania where she lives with her husband and two children, her online home can be found at CeceliaMecca.com.

She would love to hear from you.

Stay in touch:
info@ceceliamecca.com

Made in the USA
Middletown, DE
28 February 2019